La Morenita

The Story of Lupe Cordoba

Guadalupe Cordoba

PAGE PUBLISHING, INC.
Conneaut Lake, PA

First originally published by Page Publishing 2021

Cover photo by Marilyn Díaz Photography

ISBN 978-1-64334-730-1 (pbk)
ISBN 978-1-64334-759-2 (digital)

Printed in the United States of America

Contents

Foreword

THIS BOOK RELATES THE MOVING true story of Lupe Cordoba, a valiant woman from a rural area in Michoacán, Mexico, that is so small it doesn't even appear on most maps. Against all odds, she came to the United States as a very young woman with three small children and without a cent. In spite of multiple stumbling blocks in her path, she was able to painstakingly build a restaurant business that has earned accolades from California to Washington DC.

Although Lupe Cordoba had no formal schooling, she was more than capable of not only learning a great deal from the school of life but also of putting that knowledge to work for her. This story is told in the protagonist's own words. Her writing reflects the rhythms of her speech, employing a conversational tone to share her history, her successes, her failures, and her philosophy.

A very conscious effort was made to change neither Lupe Cordoba's tone nor her voice. For that reason, in the preparation of the manuscript, Anglicisms, as well as regional vocabulary and grammatical structures, were not eliminated because they are integral elements of her personal identity, forged by the forces of two cultures.

Editorial changes were made only in order to facilitate the flow of the story, to keep events in chronological order, and to clarify certain references.

This book could well serve as a guide and inspiration for many people in similar circumstances. Readers of the narrative will surely share the sorrows and happiness that Lupe Cordoba describes with so much love.

Jacqueline C. Cordova, PhD.
Editor and Translator, affiliated with Protrans

Acknowledgments

To God, FOR GIVING ME life.

To my children and my grandchildren, for being part of my life, my inspiration, the source of reconciliation, and an ocean of love.

To my parents for their love and support and for being an example to me.

To my clients for the moments of happiness and satisfaction and for their acknowledgment and acceptance.

To everyone who directly or indirectly collaborated with this story.

To Adolfo Ramirez, who contributed to the editing of this book.

CHAPTER 1

My Childhood

My Background

I WAS BORN IN A little farming settlement called La Guacatera, Michoacán, on October 10, 1942. My father, Jose Cordoba, and my mother, Maria de Jesus Valencia, named me Lupe Cordoba. There were only two of us children, me and my sister, Alvina. My parents' ancestry was as much Spanish as indigenous. My paternal grandparents, Juan Cordoba and Guadalupe Aguilar, were born in Mexico. He was of Spanish ancestry, and she came from an indigenous family. My maternal grandparents, Jose Valencia and Maria Guizar, both of Spanish descent, were born in Mexico.

My mother told me about the wars she had lived through—one involving Pancho Villa and another the Cristeros—because she was born in 1901. She said that her family was always hiding because people with guns arrived at the houses and burned them, and if there were young women, they stole them. They hid in the highest part of the mountains and in the cliffs. My father tells me that he was about eight to nine years old when the Cristeros ravaged his town. He and my grandmother often fled, since my grandfather died when my father was very young and there was no one to protect them. My father had a rooster, and he carried it in his arms and never wanted to leave it because he loved it so much. He didn't let it crow either. He always grabbed its beak so that it wouldn't crow and give away their hiding place to the Cristeros.

My mother often told us about how they suffered during those wars. In that area, there were no schools or doctors or highways to get to the nearest town. They had to go on horses or donkeys, and it was about eight or nine hours on the road from our farm to the nearest town. My parents were countryfolks. They had always lived on the farm. They had a lot of cows, pigs, and chickens. My father planted corn and beans. I remember from my childhood that my father worked with oxen to plant the fields. The first house that I remember had a tile roof and walls made of thick reeds. Corn was planted on one side behind the house, and on the other side, they had a corral where the cows were milked every morning. Beginning when I was very little, I saw that my mother worked too much. We had to grind the corn on a metate, make the tortillas by hand, and wash the clothes by hand in the river. Even as a child, I helped my mother on the farm.

My mother was an excellent cook. I remember that I paid a lot of attention to how she cooked and I always wanted to help her. She also taught me how to embroider and to knit. Those were the pastimes of the farm women. When they went into town, they took their cloth and threads to embroider pillows and napkins. I also remember when I made a dress that I sewed by hand. I was about twelve years old and had the maturity of a grown woman. From that time on, I took advantage of the time to sew. There was no other work for me to do.

My Childhood

Ever since I could think, I did a lot of daydreaming. On nights when there was a full moon, I stayed awake for long periods in my bed, thinking about all the things that I would do when I was grown-up. I would open my eyes and look at the moon from between the reeds and I would think, *The first thing that I'll do when I grow up will be to stucco the walls of the house with mud.*

I thought so much during the night that I was afraid a ghost would startle me while the others were sleeping. So that's how I grew up, dreaming day and night and being afraid of the ghosts that everybody talked about so much.

I also remember going with my grandmother to watch the pigs so they wouldn't eat the corn that was planted beside the house. I also remember the parrot that I myself taught how to talk. He always used my name when he spoke to me. He would say, "Lupita, give me a *sopita*." He also talked to the cows and whistled at the donkeys.

I loved him a lot, but one day, when I was helping my mother make tortillas, the parrot had a terrible accident. He was asking me for a *sopita* and he started to fly and then landed on the comal where we were making the tortillas. He burned his feet, and from that time on, he was never well. I doctored him, but the inevitable happened. He died, and I cried a lot. I buried him and put flowers on his grave. My mother said to me, "Don't worry so, my child. It's an animal, not a person." But I loved him a lot.

I was also given a pretty little fawn. Embracing and caressing it, I took care of it until it grew up. It was always in the house. One day, a friend of my father's arrived with a really big dog. It frightened my fawn a lot, and it went off to the hills and never returned home. Just like I did for my parrot, I cried for my little deer. After a while, I realized that somebody had killed it and eaten it without remorse. As if that weren't enough, they brought me a piece of the meat, which naturally I didn't want to eat.

From the time that I was a little girl, my mother always taught me and my sister Alvina that we had to respect other people and other people's rights and be loving with those who were dear to us. My mother always had a lot of love for everyone around her, and she was hardworking and honest. She would even go without eating in order to give food to someone else who might be hungry.

So that's the way I grew up on the farm, surrounded by animals and with my parents and my sister. I was the oldest. I remember that farmhouse so well with its reed walls and how much I pestered my mother until she told a man with a very strange name, Erasto, to stucco the walls of the house with mud. After that, I wasn't afraid at night because I couldn't see outside through the reeds.

There were a lot of trees around the house. In the rainy season, they produced a lot of fruit called *guayabillas*. We ate a lot of that fruit. There were also other trees that in the rainy season got covered with worms, really ugly ones, with black and white stripes. The trees were so full of them that the worms would dangle down, and when I walked under those trees, it seemed like they were going to fall on top of me. They frightened me so much that I still dream about them. And on the farm, there were also a lot of toads, really big ones, and iguanas and snakes and poisonous scorpions and lizards and frogs (all the animals of the countryside). I didn't like going out of the house at those times, and I cried in terror.

Our nearest neighbor lived about five miles away from that farm, and it was an uncle who had three sisters—Brigida, Maria Luisa, and Angela—and two of them were twins. We were all about the same age. We loved one another a lot. They were our only neighbors that lived close by. I remember how we went out together to the mountainside to look for the cows and how we lived on that farm.

My mother killed chickens when we wanted to eat meat. Besides that, we cut away the lard from pork to use for cooking. I remember that before killing a pig, my father went to tell all of his friends so they would come to our house so we could give them meat. That's because the pig had to be cooked the same day it was killed because on the farm there were no refrigerators—we didn't even know they existed. I first saw them when I went to California. When people wanted to eat beef., before killing the cow or the calf, they went to other farms to see how many others wanted meat. They had to sell the beef before killing the cow because if they didn't, what would they do with so much meat? My mother sliced it and put lemon and salt on it and put it out in the sun to dry. That's what a lot of people did in order to eat meat once in a while—about every six months. That's the way we lived for many years. My father went up to the highest mountain to cut pine trees and to chop small logs that we used to provide light at night before there were gas oil burners.

My childhood seems almost unbelievable to me now. I was happy and full of marvelous dreams that I was going to do a lot of wonderful things in my life. But I remember that it never entered my mind that somebody could one day help me change those dreams into reality. I always thought, *When I grow up, I'm going to work a lot, and the first things that I'm going to buy will be a closet for the clothes and a bed with a mattress because the bed I had was a cot strung with cord and covered with a straw mat.*

I also dreamed that someday I would buy a house with mosaic or tile floors because on the farm, there were only plain dirt floors that I myself tended by hand using water and mud. I didn't know about work gloves or washing machines, not to mention radios or television sets. All of our work was done by hand. I didn't know about automobiles either. I saw my first one at the age of thirteen.

I didn't get to go to school because there weren't any schools in that farm area. What little I learned, my mother taught me because she had had a home tutor teach her. When they took us to town about once a year, I remember that they mounted me on a donkey that didn't trot very smoothly. He bounced so much that I was afraid I'd fall off, and my parents had to tie me to him so I wouldn't. In town, I liked to look at the pretty houses. I remember that I stopped in front of the houses and would even stand there looking with my mouth hanging open. I thought, *Someday I'll be able to have a pretty house like this.*

I've loved flowers since I was a little girl. I had a lot of flowers in my house. And do you know what I used for flowerpots? Old pots, broken pitchers, and useless old cans! That's where I planted my flowers. I know that nobody is going to believe it, but I carried the water from the river in buckets in order to water the plants. The river was more than half a mile away from my house. The road was narrow and surrounded by trees on both sides, all the way from the house to the river.

Jesus and Jose Cordoba wedding picture
Lupe's parents, 1938

I also liked to paint the walls of my house with colors. What do you think I used for paint on that little farm? I used colored soil that I myself brought from the highest part of the mountain on a donkey that my parents had. I used to beg my mother to take me there so I could bring back the soil. On that mountain, you could find soil in shades of red, yellow, pale blue, and white. I remember it very well. To mix the paint, I would put water in a bucket, along with the soil of the color I was going to use. I would stir the soil well with the water and then I would paint with a piece of cloth that I soaked in the mixture. That's how I made drawings on the walls of my house. And do you know how old I was when I began to do that work around the house? Eleven! It didn't matter how ugly the houses were where I lived. I painted them and put in pretty gardens all by myself. I also wanted to learn to read and write. And I succeeded, although not perfectly. I also wanted to learn dressmaking, and I did.

That's how my first thirteen years were spent. And I was thinking that I would get married soon because I always heard the grown women and many old people saying that a girl should be married before she was eighteen. Because if she didn't, she would be an old maid, and I didn't want to be an old maid. I always paid attention when they talked about girls who didn't get married and about those who got married and quit taking care of themselves and got fat and ugly. I also heard that that's why men left them and went off with other women and that rich men got maids for their wives, and later the maids became the men's lovers. Well, all of those things stuck in my mind forever, and that's the reason I have never had a maid in my house. That hasn't helped to straighten out my life at all.

Love Letters

The day came when a man wrote me a love letter asking if I wanted to be his girlfriend. At that time, I wasn't yet fourteen, and he was seventeen years older than me. I still didn't know how to write well; I was barely learning. So I took the letter to a cousin who was older than me. She read me the letter and said, "Honey, don't even think about loving that man. He's way too old for you. You're still a little girl."

She wrote the answer for me, saying no. After that, I had two other suitors, or so I thought. But I remember that when we talked, it was always at the river's edge, hidden from my mother and father, and the only thing we did was look into each other's eyes and laugh for a few minutes. We had nothing to say.

Because I had the idea in mind to learn dressmaking, I begged my father to buy me a sewing machine and to leave me in town with a dressmaker so she could give me lessons. I insisted so much that he finally gave me permission. They bought me the machine and they left me in town with one of my mother's married brothers. The dressmaker who was going to give me lessons lived across the street.

My aunt and uncle protected me as if I were a jewel. I couldn't go out alone for any reason. In that town, there was a garden, or rather, a plaza. Every Sunday, the town girls walked around in the plaza, and the boys gave them flowers and threw confetti in their hair. To me, it all looked very pretty, but my aunt and uncle didn't let me walk around, or if I did, it was with them. Well, there in the dressmaker's house, I met a boy. His name was Eduardo Gonzalez. He was very good-looking, and I liked him a lot. But I was so naive—such a country girl! I barely knew how to read. They didn't even let us read a magazine or anything that would help us to wake up a little. So I thought, if that boy asked me to be his girlfriend, I would marry him as soon as he asked.

But one day, I saw that he was looking a little sad, and when I asked what was wrong, he answered that his girlfriend had left him. I tried to cheer him up and said that there were a lot of girls around. He also lived on a farm with his parents and brothers and sisters, but he came into town and to the dressmaker's house frequently.

Well, the moment I was waiting for arrived. One day, he came into town, and I was alone in the dressmaker's shop for a minute, and he asked if I wanted to be his girlfriend. I was startled and answered that I would like to think about it a little while before saying yes. Well, we became boyfriend and girlfriend, but we were only able to see each other occasionally. There were only a few times that we could secretly talk a little because if my aunt and uncle caught on, there would be trouble!

At that time, my father came into town and took me back to the farm. Then my suitor came to see me there at the farm—on a horse. I had already told him where I lived. He spent the whole day hidden among the trees beside the river until I went to get water for the house. And then he came where I was, by the river. My mother always timed us as we went back and forth to the river. That day, he asked me to marry him and said his family would come to ask for my hand the next week. Just then, I could see my mother very close to us in the trees. It really shocked me, and he had to run away immediately. When she got home, my mother told my father that I had gone to the river to look for a cow named La Guacamaya, and that instead of the cow, I had found a Brahma bull. In spite of the fact that she gave me a good scolding, I couldn't help laughing—what she said seemed so funny. Well, after that, they didn't let me go down to the river or anyplace alone. What do you think of that?

Getting Married with Blinders On

The following week, Eduardo's parents came to ask for my hand. My parents didn't want me to get married for anything in the world. But when a person wants something badly enough, nobody or nothing can get in the way. My poor mother! I was the only daughter still at home. Adolfina, a little girl that my parents adopted when her mother died in childbirth, was still at home, but she was only seven years old and couldn't help my mother much with the chores. Now I think how thoughtless children are to their parents! It doesn't matter to us that they love us and take care of us!

Besides, my mother was the most long-suffering woman in the world. She lived all her life on the farm, working very hard doing the household chores and feeding the animals and taking care of them. I was the only one who helped her, and now I was going to be married. My mother gave me a lot of advice. She would say to me, "Look at how your sister Alvina is living. She was only fourteen years old when she got married, and then they took her to live on another farm that was even farther away from our town."

It was really horrible there, and they were hardly married before they were mad at each other, even during the wedding. She was very young, and Juan, my brother-in-law, was a hermit, and they never went to town or mingled with people who weren't members of the family. And besides, he hit my sister for any reason. My father wanted to take her away from him. They were like wild animals with no manners or respect. My parents didn't want my sister to get married for anything in the world, but she didn't want to understand, just like me. Now I think the truth is that I really didn't like our farm. It was too lonely. The only friends I had close by had also gotten married, and I didn't want to be an old maid. Finally, my parents threw up their hands and gave me their permission to marry.

A Pink Wedding

Well, I got married three months after Eduardo's family asked for my hand and without our knowing each other enough to make such a big decision. I was young and naive. I had no idea what marriage was all about. Everything that I thought turned out exactly the opposite. I'll never forget the day of that wedding. Eduardo sent over a horse with a new saddle and a man and his wife to bring me from the ranch into town. Those people were going to be our wedding godparents. Then my father came to hand me over, and my mother stayed on the farm. I can still see her in my mind. She blessed me with her eyes full of tears. She was much stronger than my father.

Well, we got to the town and the next day had a civil ceremony. We had to wait three days for the religious wedding. To my father, it seemed as though I were in my coffin, dead. He cried as if I really had died. Nothing could console him.

My wedding dream was to be dressed in white with an embroidered dress and everything. Unfortunately, it turned out just the opposite. They dressed the groom in white and me in pink. The groom's mother said that the dress had to be pink because if it were white, I couldn't wear it again and it was a big expense. When I saw the dress, I couldn't help feeling sad.

"Why pink?" I said to my future mother-in-law.

She answered, "Oh, honey, pink is very pretty, and you can't wear white again."

Well, that made me feel very sad inside, but I wasn't brave enough to say that I didn't want it. And so the hour arrived; I married one day in January of 1958, and my father could see that I wasn't completely happy. He said to me, "Honey, if you don't want to get married, I'll take you away right now and you don't have to do it."

But I thought that I had already given my word and that it was too late to go back on it. I was already married in a civil ceremony. Well, when I got to the church and I saw him dressed in white, I almost fainted. Although I was a naive fool, I thought that topped it! If I was the one who wanted to be dressed in white, why was he in white and I in pink? That was incredible enough, but it still wasn't the end. After leaving the church, we had to go and sign papers at another place in the same building. And since I wasn't accustomed to wearing high-heeled shoes and he wasn't holding my hand, I don't know how, but one heel of a shoe got stuck in a little hole in the floor and I fell down, and the people who were with us just stood around laughing. That really did me in. I wanted the earth to swallow me up! We got to the reception, and I felt like I was dying inside. My father didn't stop crying. He loved me so much and didn't want to lose such a big part of this life. After the meal and a small toast, we were ready to go on our honeymoon, which for me, instead of honey, seemed to be of terror because of everything that was happening to me. My heart broke when I saw how sad and worried my father was. I will never in my life forget that day.

Honeymoon

Well, we got to Guadalajara, Jalisco. It was the first time I had seen so many people and such a large city with so many lights. For me, it was all very new. We were only there for four days, but we couldn't enjoy ourselves at all because wherever we went, we got lost. Neither he nor I had ever been farther than the small town where we met. Then we went to Uruapan, Michoacán. That city was smaller. We were there for four days. But what was waiting for me as a new bride didn't even enter my mind. Ten days later, we got back to the town where we were going to live, a place called Aguililla, Michoacán, Mexico.

When we arrived in Aguililla, I found out that we were going to live in the same house with the dressmaker and that my husband didn't own a bed for us to sleep in. We had to sleep on the floor. We had no money—absolutely nothing. Although during my childhood I had lived on a farm far from town, my parents had beds for us to sleep in, even though they were just cots. A cot during my childhood was very different from a tile floor as a newly married woman! Later, my husband and I bought a bed, but we had to wait two months for it to be delivered. Meanwhile, I was very uncomfortable.

My husband then told me that he had to go and plant on a farm that was about three hours away from town and that we had to go live on a farm for a while. But we had to live under a tree because there was no house! There would be a straw roof. Well, that news almost killed me. It filled me with terror to think of living under a tree with all the animals of the countryside, with snakes, iguanas, lizards, toads, and frogs. But what could I do? I had to do whatever my husband said. I had sworn, "Until death do us part." During that time, my father came to see me. He arrived and embraced me and started to cry, as always, and he told me that the family house on the farm was very desolate without me. It broke my heart, but what could I do? When it came time to go to bed, I wanted the earth to swallow me up. Where was my father going to sleep? Besides, he would find out that I didn't have a bed, and that's the way it was. He said to me, "But, daughter, what's going on here? Don't you have a bed to sleep in?"

I answered that Eduardo had bought one but that it hadn't been delivered. My father couldn't control the pain he felt when he saw his daughter in such complete poverty. And the next day, he went and bought me a folding cot made with canvas. Well, after seeing him so worried, I didn't tell him anything about how I was going to live under a tree. So about a month after getting married, we went to live on that farm.

Under a Heavenly Roof

Under a large tree beside a river, I cried black tears of fear and sadness because there were snakes and lots of iguanas and lizards, toads and frogs, and river scorpions. The tree was very big, very green, beautiful, and leafy. Its shade was big enough to be like a roof. We used stones and mud to build a sort of stove so I could cook and make tortillas. My husband got me a grinding stone to grind the corn and make the dough for the tortillas. Well, there under that tree, he made a straw fence to put around the bed that my father had given me. That was my refuge. Whenever I saw an iguana or lizard coming close to where I was, I chased it away and got up on the bed.

There was also a road traveled by many people who were going to the Aguililla, which was the only nearby town. People from the area where I had lived with my parents passed by on horseback. When I saw people passing by, I hid. I didn't want anybody to see me. It made me too ashamed. I didn't want my parents to know where I was living. I had to wash in the river. And you know how I ironed the clothes? I took a mouthful of water, sprayed it out, and then smoothed the clothes out with my hands. That way, they weren't so wrinkled. During those two months of hell living with a tree for a house, I was alone most of the day. My husband worked almost all day long, planting.

Well, one fine day, my father arrived where I was. I almost fainted when I saw him. I'll never forget the sadness I saw in his face. The first thing he said to me was, "Oh, daughter, how can they have you living here?"

At that moment, my husband arrived, and my father said straight out, "You're going to take my daughter to a house right away. If you don't, then I'm going to take her home with me to my house and you won't see her again until you have a house to live in."

Well, my husband had no choice. He took me back to town. By that time, I looked like a corpse. People didn't recognize me after those two months had gone by. We didn't have anything to eat but stewed beans and tortillas—nothing else.

Well, I had studied dressmaking. I had learned to make dresses, and my father had given me the sewing machine, but my husband didn't want me to sew for strangers because he thought he had to support me. But we didn't have a cent, not even one to buy a liter of milk, until I decided that I had to sew. The fields that my husband had planted wouldn't produce any money for about six months. I told my husband, "I have to work sewing clothes. I'm not going to die of hunger. What did I study dressmaking for?"

Well, even though he didn't agree, he had to accept the idea.

Life in Town

The dressmaker who had taught me lived in the same house, and she gave me some of the work she had. In a very short time, I had my own customers. Now I was earning some money, even if it was just enough to buy food. I was now providing a lot of help. I began to fix up the house a little because it was very neglected. Apparently, the dressmaker didn't like it when I fixed up the house. She would say, "Why are you working so hard? It's not even your house."

So I painted it myself with some white powder called lime. And I fixed up the kitchen too. I wanted my husband, Eduardo, to feel proud of me. When my in-laws came to visit, they were very surprised. They thought their son had painted the house. When I told them that I had done it, they said, "What do you mean you did it?"

I answered that I had really done it. I also told them that on the farm, I painted my house and made drawings with different colors of soil. They were really surprised and pleased with me.

In that little town, almost everybody knew everybody else. I can still see the church and the streets in my mind. The church in that town was on a tall hill, with the rest of the town around it. All the streets were cobblestone—sidewalks and streets—all of them, even around the church. There was also the traditional plaza with gardens around it, and in the middle, there was a bandstand where an orchestra played on Sundays. There were also bands when there were celebrations, and all the young people walked around. The couples who were seriously dating would get together in the plaza to talk. It all seemed so beautiful to me. Early in the morning, all of us women went to the mill to grind the cooked corn that we used to make the tortillas. And every day, all of the people in town went shopping in the morning for what would be eaten during the day because there were no refrigerators there. Every day it was the same routine of buying the day's necessities. Also, in that town, there was no work for women except as dressmakers or servants. There was no electric light during the time I lived there. There was a small electric plant that barely gave enough light for the plaza.

My First Baby

Well, the moment arrived when I discovered I was pregnant. Since we were so poor, how could I go to the doctor? I had to see a *curandera*. Oh God, I was really thin! I looked like a toothpick and I really got sick during the pregnancy. I couldn't eat anything. Even my husband nauseated me. There was a grocery store four houses away from mine, and at that time, there were some very popular songs: "Monedita," "Diente de Oro," and "Gema." They were played so often that I vomited just from hearing them. They not only played those songs all day long, but the loudspeakers at the side of the road made it seem as if the music were being played right in my house! I didn't get rid of my nausea until after my daughter Gloria was born.

That is how the first year passed, and my daughter Gloria was born on February 11, 1959. It was quite an experience for me, since I had never taken care of a baby before. She cried a lot when she was small. She didn't let me sleep, and I cried right along with her. At that time, my daughter was my father's pride and joy, and he gave me a big surprise.

Home Sweet Home

My father told me that he was going to give me some money so that my husband could build me a house on his vacant lot in town. That's how my golden dream was fulfilled. They built me the house, you know, I can see it in my mind. It had only one very large room and a door facing the street and a little porch at the back of the house. On the porch, I had my kitchen with a grinding stone and a hearth where I cooked. At one side of the room, we had the beds, and on the other side, we had the sewing machines. The door was right in the middle. And the other door opened to the garden in the back. I myself planted everything in that garden because in that town, you couldn't buy flowering plants. We had to plant the seeds and tend the rose branches that my relatives or friends gave me in order to make them grow. By myself, I made sure that the branches took hold, and that's the way we made the gardens grow.

By then, I was pregnant again, but now I had my house with its gardens and my own work. I was now giving dressmaking classes to other girls in my home. My second child arrived on July 14, 1960. He was a little boy named Uriel. The truth is, I don't know how I did it all. I washed and ironed the clothes. I cooked and took care of the children. Besides this, I worked at dressmaking. When I had a lot of sewing, I worked until two o'clock in the morning with a gas oil burner fastened to the side of the sewing machine because there was no good light in town. Time kept passing by, and another daughter, Esmeralda, was born on December 13, 1962. Three years of marriage and three children. My husband had opened a small grocery store, and with my dressmaking, we were happy. We had conquered poverty, at least a little.

Bad Luck Comes in Bunches

In January, we got the news in town that a certain number of men could arrange residency documents to go to California for the sum of five thousand Mexican pesos. My husband signed up, and an uncle lent him money, so he sold the store and went with the whole group to Empalme, Sonora, Mexico. It really made me very sad to be left alone with three children and all the responsibility. I was very young, but everything that was happening to me was making me stronger. He was stuck in Empalme, Sonora, for three months, arranging for his passport. He wrote to me very often and would ask me to borrow money to send him because he didn't have any, not even for food. And since bad luck comes in bunches, I had the same problem. People weren't paying me for the sewing on time, and all I could do was cry and pray and ask God not to forget us in those difficult moments.

One day, a rich lady came to my house to ask if I knew anyone who washed and ironed clothes because her servant had left her. Well, immediately I said yes, that I did know a woman who would do it but that she was not in right at the moment. That's because I was ashamed to tell her that I was going to do it myself. I did that work for about four months. There were eight people in the woman's family, and I washed and ironed all their clothes. By then, I had calluses from washing clothes, but I never told her I did the work. In order to quit, I said that the woman would no longer do the washing.

By then, my husband was in California and he was sending me money. But I was very afraid that he was going to fall in love with another woman in California and that he would forget me and his children. Two years had gone by, and he hadn't returned. I had prayed to God so much that he could get his passport, and God made the dream a reality. But I was still afraid. Suddenly, something terrible and unexpected happened. My son, Uriel, died instantly after taking a pill that my mother-in-law gave him. That was too much pain for me. My parents came from their farm, and they helped me a lot, but it really took a lot out of me.

Setting Out for El Norte

And that's why my husband returned. But now, he wasn't the same person who had gone to California. Now I was too ugly and very skinny and too countrified for him. It seemed as if he had gone to another planet. At twelve noon, he had to have his plate ready and on the table, and if not, there was a quarrel. He was no longer loving toward his children. He was very cold with them and with me too. I ate in an ugly way, I walked in an ugly way, everything that I was or did was ugly to him. He was home for two months, and I only saw him at mealtime, and sometimes he even ate out. I heard him talk a lot about the California girls with his friends, saying they were very pretty and very "easy." And here I had thought that I was all the woman he needed. Now he made me feel just like a dog.

He told me—my husband did—that I should never even think that one day he would take me to California. That he was never going to do it. And do you know what I did? I just cried and cried. I cried buckets. Everything had fallen apart for me. I had lost a child and I was going to lose my husband. I felt such deep pain in my heart that I thought I was going to die. He went back to California as if nothing was wrong. Then I thought, if I were to die, what would my two daughters do without a father and a mother?

Then I went to church and knelt before a statue of Christ. With tears running down my face, I went to plead with him that if my husband were going to leave me and my daughters, his heart would soften and he would arrange documents for us so that I could go far away where nobody knew me. As always, God heard my prayer. Up until now, God had never abandoned us. I give thanks to him every day of my life. My husband agreed to get us papers, but it wasn't easy.

He sent me the letters, and I had to go with my two small daughters to Mexico City federal district to put in the application. It was such a big city! When I got to the embassy with all the documents, they turned me down because the documents were incomplete. I had to go back to my town to get what was missing. It was difficult because when my husband left Mexico for the second time, he left me pregnant. I was just like a rabbit! Anyway, I returned to Mexico City with all the correct documents. They told me I could pick up the passports in three months. Then my son, Rafael, was born on June 6, 1964, and that led to another problem. They called me from Mexico City to go and pick up the passports, but I couldn't go. I had to change the appointment. Then when I got to the American Embassy again, they said I had to prove the baby was mine. I had to go back to my town again to get papers for the baby, and my husband had to be present. Finally, everything got arranged. Now I had hopes of saving my marriage.

We arrived in Merced, California, in September of 1964. On the one hand, I was happy because my husband had brought us with him, but on the other, it really hurt to leave all my friends and, most of all, my parents whom I loved so much. Leaving them was very hard for me.

Desolation in California

In California, I really felt naive and ignorant. I didn't understand one word of English. Then a real struggle began. My husband worked with some ranch owners who planted lots of fields of chili peppers, tomatoes, and sweet potatoes. They gave us a house, rent-free. They also gave me work in the fields. It was very difficult for me and my children to get used to living in this country. My daughters, Gloria and Esmeralda, spent all their time watching television and taking care of the baby, Rafael, who was only a few months old. They also missed our town in Mexico very much because there they had a lot of little friends to play with and they were free, while here it was like a prison for them. When they saw other children in the laundromats or the grocery store, they would look at them longingly. They wanted so badly to play with them.

At that time, there weren't as many Latinos in this country as there are now. My daughter Gloria was the one who suffered most from this change because she was only five years old. She'll never forget the first day that she went to school because it was very embarrassing for her. She wanted to go to the bathroom and didn't know how to tell the teacher, and she wet her underpants. That was very hard for her.

I remember very well that the teachers were very strict about how the children dressed for school. Once, my daughter wore the same dress two days in a row. It wasn't dirty because when she got home from school, I had her change her clothes so she could put the dress on the next day. Right away, they sent me a note from school saying that the child couldn't wear the same dress to class two days in a row. Now they don't have such strict rules as they did thirty years ago.

I think my daughter Gloria was one of those who suffered a lot the first year of school here in California because of the language. I remember that at first, she was very nervous and afraid to go to school. And besides, who was going to help her? My husband didn't know any English, and I knew less. I had just arrived. I felt just like the girls. I didn't know anybody. My husband had some friends and work buddies. At that time, he was nice-looking and very hardworking but one of those men who really humiliate their women—men who think they are in charge of everything and whose wives have no value. The only thing that matters is what they say.

The first year, I worked in the fields and packing houses. I turned my whole check over to my husband. All I did was sign it. I never had a cent. The second year, I couldn't work in the fields because the sun gave me really terrible headaches. Then a friend at work told me that some of her friends worked for Foster Farms and that they were accepting applications; and if I got the job, her friends would give me a ride since they lived near my house. So that's what happened. I applied and then got work at Foster Farms in Livingston, California.

They paid better there than in the fields, and since I knew how to cut with shears, it wasn't difficult for me to cut up chickens. The supervisor even thought I had experience with that kind of work.

I had been working in the plant for a year by then, and the friends that gave me a ride every day always went to the bank to cash their checks. Often, they went to the stores to buy clothes and things, and I just watched them. They would say, "Why don't you cash your check, Lupe? Don't you feel like buying anything?"

I answered, "Of course, but I can't. My husband would get mad."

"But how can you be so dumb? It's really your check!"

But my husband had told me, "It'll never be your money. You have to turn over the whole check to me every week. You're not going to be like the women around here who spend their money on foolishness."

So he gave me a quarter every night to buy coffee at work, because I always took my lunch. He bought me clothes that *he* liked, not what *I* liked. We had been in California for more than two years, and he never took us anywhere except to buy food or wash clothes. He treated me badly for no reason, as if I were garbage with no value. My children hardly had any clothes, and I didn't either. He kept all the money in the bank.

One payday, as always, the friends who gave me a ride went to the bank to cash their checks. They said to me, "Lupe, don't be such a fool. Cash your check and buy something for yourself and your kids."

I was tempted, so I cashed the check. We got to a store that had very pretty clothes for children and adults. I knew what was in store for me, but I bought a dress for each girl, anyway. I've never forgotten the colors. The dresses were cream-colored with pink and yellow flowers, and I bought a little blue-and-green suit for my son. I bought myself a gold-colored dress, very pretty, of course. I'll never forget that dress as long as I live. When I got home, my husband wasn't there. My daughters were very happy with their dresses.

I worked at night, and when I got home, I went directly to the kitchen to make food for my children and my husband. As soon as he walked in the door, he saw the girls with the new dresses. Well, I really wish that he hadn't come home. That day, we had the biggest fight in my life. He treated me like garbage, and I answered that it was my money. He even hit me very hard in the face in front of the children and told me that he didn't love me at all.

CHAPTER 2

Abandoned

All Alone

RIGHT THEN, MY HUSBAND TOLD me we were going to Mexico to get divorced immediately and that he didn't want to live with a woman like me. After seven and a half years, that was the end of the marriage. He bought a station wagon, and we went to Mexico. My mother had died about six months earlier on the farm where I was born. Nobody even told me about it until they had buried her. I still hadn't gotten over my sorrow, especially since I knew I would never see my mother again. And to top it off, my husband was going to desert me and my children.

When we got to Aguililla, what do you think happened? My husband left us in the house we had there. He immediately took off for his parents' home. He took off and didn't leave me one cent to buy food for me and my children. I felt like I was in a deep hole with no way out. I couldn't believe what was happening. It really seemed impossible to me. What was I going to tell my father and all of my relatives in the town? And my husband's parents? I didn't know what to tell them because everybody that knew us used to say he was the best man in the world. That we were an ideal couple. How could I ask for a loan, since we had just come from California? Nobody knew what was going on between us.

The day after we arrived, a very dear cousin named Maria Alcazar came to visit. She was twelve years older than me, and she thought of me as a daughter. We had spent a lot of time together on the farm where I was born, and I had to tell her the whole truth about what was happening in my marriage. She hugged me, and the two of us cried about my misfortune. She lent me money to buy food.

On the third day, my father arrived, and all I could do was cry. My father was so happy to see me that he told me I was his favorite daughter. How could I tell him what was happening to me? Then he asked about my husband, Eduardo. I answered that he was with his parents, but I couldn't fool my father. I had to tell him the truth. It almost gave him a heart attack.

As if that wasn't enough, my husband arrived at that moment. My father wanted to kill him. Eduardo told my father I was like a mule, and that's why he was leaving me. How cruel! My father got very angry. I was afraid that something awful would happen. My father yelled at my husband and told him to give me the money that I had earned and said it wasn't fair for him to keep everything, that he should do it for his children's sake. My husband answered that he wasn't going to give me a penny and that if I wanted money, I should return to California to work. He shouted at my father that he wasn't going to give me money so that I could attract another man, even if my father and my relatives killed him. My husband ran out quickly, and he took all the money with him. The only thing I had left were the check stubs from what I earned in the fields and at the Foster Farms plant.

Then I went to see the authorities about putting in a claim against him so he would give me some of what was really mine. But from there, they sent me to another town, to Apatzingán, Michoacán, to put in the claim. So I went, with my three kids and the check stubs, to Apatzingán. First, I went to the bank where he told me he had deposited all the money. I spoke to the bank manager, but it was no use. The bank manager told me, "All you can do is go to police headquarters and file a claim. That's all you can do."

When I left the bank with my children, my husband's parents were outside, crying and begging me to please not sue him. He could kill me if I did that. He had told them that if I filed a claim against him, he would kill me. They said they would give me money to take the children back to California. So I didn't do anything because I felt so sorry for them. I returned to my house in Aguililla and sold everything in it, and what I didn't sell, I gave away. Although we had built the house with money that my father gave me, my husband didn't want to give me the deed or let me have my share of the house. He told his parents that the house would be for the children when they grew up. That was just a lie! He sold it very quickly without even thinking of his children. Then his parents gave me money for the return trip by bus to California. At that time, it cost five thousand Mexican pesos.

A Woman's Courage and Determination

Before leaving, I took my father to Mexico City so he could apply for immigration papers and come to California with us, but in the consulate, they told him that it would take three months to get a visa. My father never went to school. He didn't even know how to sign his name. I had to hold his hand and guide him to sign all the documents. I had no choice but to go back to California alone with the children. Gloria, the eldest, was seven years old, and Rafael, the youngest, was two. Well, thirty years later, I ask myself how I could have been brave enough to leave Mexico for the United States alone with three small children. I looked like their sister. It took us three days and three nights on the bus to get to Tijuana.

I had some surprises on the road. In a town called Guaymas, Sonora, we found out that the bridge over a large river was falling down. Neither cars nor buses could cross. Cars had to stop, and the people had to cross the bridge on foot to wait for another bus to pick them up on the other side. It was so hot there that nobody could stand it, especially the children. I had practically no money, and the children wanted to eat and drink sodas every few minutes. I would buy them something, and in a little while, bathed in sweat, they wanted something else. There were no trees where a person could stand in the shade. There was only a little store where hardly five people could fit, and that space was for those buying something. I cried there, along with my children. Every few minutes along the road, the kids wanted to go to the bathroom. And I kept saying, "Mr. Chauffeur, please stop the bus. My children want to go to the bathroom."

The driver would stop, and I would take them off the bus to take care of their problem, only to discover that they didn't want to do anything because there was no bathroom. It was out in the desert, and there weren't even any trees to hide behind. My children said to me, "Not here, please. Mommy, not here, please."

And I said to them, "Well, you have to. There's nowhere else."

At that time, the buses in Mexico didn't have bathrooms, so the bus had to stop every few minutes. If it wasn't some people, it was others who had the same need.

We finally got to Tijuana, Baja California. I was praying in my thoughts, begging God to take care of us. We arrived as dirty as pigs. There was no way to get a hotel if I didn't have any money to pay for it. I hardly had enough to buy the kids something to eat. Well, near the terminal, there was a restaurant. I went and asked a woman if she would give me permission to change our clothes in the restaurant's restroom. After we changed, I asked her if she knew of anyone who could give us a ride to Merced, California, because I didn't have any money for us to go by bus. That good woman told me to go to the border to ask because I could find someone there who took people to California. She told me where to look. Then I got a taxi to take us to the border. The driver left us with our suitcases at the entrance to the border.

The Uncertain Road

Among the people I met at the border was a man who agreed to transport us and wait to get paid until we arrived in Merced. I think he felt sorry for me. Now I ask myself how I could have gotten into a car with somebody that I didn't even know, especially with how worried I was that something bad would happen to me and my children. During the whole trip, I prayed and asked God to take care of us and not let that man do anything bad to us.

Sad but True

Thank God, we arrived in Merced safe and sound. I had a key to the house that my husband's boss had given us. There were two bosses—a Portuguese man and an American. They were very good to us. The house was very near their office. I left the children in the house and went to ask the boss, who was named Jose, to lend me some money. I was lucky enough to find him in the office. When he saw me, he said, "What's going on, Lupe? Your husband is working. Do you want me to tell him that you're here?"

Well, in all my sorrow, I had to tell him the truth that I needed him to lend me money to pay the man who had brought us from Tijuana. And I told him that my husband had left us in Mexico without one penny. Then Jose went and paid the man who brought us. And then he said to me, "But your husband is working here on the ranch. I'll bring him right over."

I could see by the look in his eyes how bad he felt about my news. With tears in his eyes, he went and brought Eduardo, my husband. Then he took away his keys to the station wagon and gave them to me. He said, "You're keeping the station wagon, and he's leaving my ranch this very minute! I don't want him here one more minute!"

I didn't want the station wagon, but Jose said to me, "Lupe, please keep it."

But I was very foolish, and besides, I didn't even know how to start a car. What was I going to do with the station wagon? At that moment, Eduardo grabbed the keys and drove away in the station wagon. My daughter Esmeralda, who was four and a half years old, ran after him, and he said cruelly, "Get out of here! Go back to your mother!"

She came back crying. Then Mr. Silva just looked at me and shook his head. He said, "Do you want me to call the police? They'll find him right away."

But I didn't want him to do that. I thought that then he would really kill me, and what would my children do then?

With God's Help

I don't know how I kept going. I was very young and had absolutely nothing (just my children, my hands, and my feet). But

I felt incredible strength to fight and show the world that one day, with the help of God, I would triumph. Then Mr. Silva said to me, "Look, Lupe, I can let you stay and live in the house as long as you want, but how will you get around without a car? It's impossible, really! And then with the kids…what are you going to do?"

I answered that I was going to talk to one of my husband's friends who lived in Livingston to see if he knew of anybody who could rent me a room or share an apartment. I was going to keep on working at Foster Farms in Livingston. Then he said to me, "You can stay here in this house as long as you want. But if you go, take the things you need from the house. They're yours."

He also gave me a little money that he never would let me pay back.

Without a Clue

At that time, I couldn't even imagine all that the future would bring. The good thing is that God never deserts us as long as we don't forget about Him. I phoned my husband's friend, and he got me a room close to the chicken plant with another friend. I could walk to work, and since I worked at night, she could take care of the kids. I showed up at the job to say I was ready to start working. Before going to Mexico, I had asked for a leave of absence. Well, imagine my surprise when I found out that I had to wait two or three weeks for them to place me! Then Lupe really began to cry buckets of tears! What was I going to do? Then the woman I shared the apartment with consoled me, saying, "Look, Lupe, you're a legal resident. Let's go get some government aid for you and the children while you're not working. I'll take you."

So we went, kids and all, to Merced, California. They denied me aid because I didn't know where my children's father was. At that time, they were stricter than they are now. Then I said, "I think we're really going to die of hunger now!"

My friend worked in a field, harvesting grapes. She said, "Lupe, don't worry so much. Come work in the fields with me."

I said, "And the children?"

"Well, you just take them with you," she said.

There was really no other choice. We went to the fields to pick grapes. Gloria, my oldest daughter, took care of the little ones. We worked about seven or eight hours a day. We walked home like monkeys, me and the kids. And do you know how much I earned? I'll never forget! It was about five or six dollars a day. But at that time, at least it was enough to buy a little food.

Three weeks later, they called me to work at the plant. That was a big relief! But as the saying goes, "When a tree falls, everybody wants to make firewood of it." I was now the talk of the town for a lot of people. I had some cousins who lived close to me. Out of respect for them, I'm not going to mention their names. One of them was a married woman. One day, I was coming home from the store with the children, carrying the youngest and a bag of groceries. Her husband felt sorry for me and gave me a ride home. Later I found out that he had a big fight with his wife about helping me. He never offered me a ride again.

People said that all the men I talked to were my lovers. That's because in all of the families on my mother's side, nobody ever talked about separating from one's husband, and it was a very big family. On my father's side of the family, it was the same—marriage until death do us part. I was the first to break that barrier. It was a real scandal. Nobody had even a drop of consideration for me. One relative sent a letter to Mexico to one of my beloved cousins, who thought of me almost as a daughter. It was a letter that said awful things about me, including that I was the most shameless woman on earth and that I went to the fields to flirt with all the men and that my husband had left me for that reason. When my cousin sent me the letter to read, I wanted to die. I couldn't believe such viciousness.

Disillusionments and Surprises

My destiny was now decided, and only God knew what it would be. I think I was in love with love. At that time, I couldn't believe that all men would only hurt me, especially men who seemed good and kind. One day, I went to the doctor to buy something to keep me from getting pregnant if I should happen to slip up one day, since there was a young man whom I really liked. When he asked me to go out, I said to myself, "Well, I'm not going to be alone for the rest of my life. I have to get to know a man. They're not all bad. There must be some good ones."

But I couldn't even imagine how my future with men would be. They only wanted to play with my sentiments. Nobody wanted to make a life with a woman who already had children. Just spend some time and enjoy themselves with her or try to take advantage of her—that's all. Well, I went out with that young man. He wasn't married, and I wanted to get to know him. I said to myself, *Well, they talk about me, anyway, even when I don't go out with anybody.*

We worked at the same place. By that time, I had rented a little house and I had become friendly with the neighbors. They were nice people. I had bought a bed, a dining room table, a refrigerator, and a living room set—all secondhand and very cheap, but at least, we now had a place to sit down. Well, what happened with the handsome young man who invited me to go out? The first few times, I took the children along with me. Later I left them with a friend at my house because they wouldn't even let me see the movie. Well, after I had been going out with him for about three months, somebody told me he had a girlfriend and that if I wanted, I could go see for myself. So I went. And yes, it was true. There he was, the handsome young man, holding hands with her. I thought the earth would swallow me up. How could that be? He had said he loved me. Well, I went over to him. All I said to him was, "Hello. Is this the way you treat everybody?"

And he turned red and told me, "Go away, please."

And I said to him, "You better believe it," and he never came looking for me again.

What was the next big surprise that fate had prepared for me? That I was pregnant and I hadn't even realized it! When the doctor told me, I almost fainted.

"It's not possible. I'm taking pills," I told him.

"That's not true, or else they didn't help you," he answered.

"Oh my god! What am I going to do? People will eat me up alive!"

Well, I cried, and nothing could console me. The children would say, "What's the matter, Mommy? Why are your crying? Are you sick?"

And I would say to them, "Nothing's the matter."

But they kept insisting. "Why are you crying?"

"Something hurts me a lot."

The oldest, Gloria, said to me, "Should I make you some tea?"

"No, honey, it'll go away."

So I kept on working, but I was always thinking, *I have to get away from here. If I don't, people will eat me up alive.*

My First Car

Along with everything else, life was becoming harder and harder without a car. My father was about to arrive from Mexico, and I wanted to be able to drive him around. I had a friend whom I could talk to about everything that was happening to me. We were very close. She said, "Lupe, you can't kill yourself. Think of your children. I'm going to talk to my father and see if he'll help you buy a car. You'll have time to learn how to drive. Anyway, your pregnancy won't show while you're learning."

That friend was named Teresa Sepeda. And that's what she did. The next day at work, her father said to me, "Lupe, I'll be happy to sign for you so you can buy a car."

After work, we went to look at cars. He asked me, "How much money do you have?"

I answered, "A hundred and fifty dollars. Do you think that I can buy a car with such a small down payment?"

He said, "I think so. A little used car, yeah, you can."

In spite of everything, God was with me. We went looking for cars. There was one for five hundred dollars, a green Ford Falcon. How can I ever forget my first car? That good man, Jose Sepeda, signed for me, and they let me buy it on time payments. Can you believe it? I didn't even know how to drive; I didn't even have a license. At that moment, I thought that even if there are heartless men, there are also good-hearted and very kind people.

Then I called my cousin, Manuel Valencia, to ask him to do me the favor of going with my friend's father to bring home the car I had bought. When they brought the car home, my children were really happy to see it. Then my cousin taught me how to start the engine and how to move backward and forward. He also taught me how to use the signals and he gave me some other instructions. After he left, I put my kids in the car and I went to learn how to drive in the streets, because there wasn't any traffic. I drove around a little, and when I went back home, my neighbor was very worried, praying that nothing bad would happen to me. She came running out and said, "But Lupe, how could you take the kids with you when you don't even know how to drive? Aren't you afraid of killing yourself and them?"

I answered, "I'm not afraid because if anything happens to us, we'll all go together."

But still, I took all the precautions that I could. I stopped at every corner, even when there was no stop sign. There was a fence in front of my house, and every time I went out, I broke off a little piece of it until I had knocked it all down. But I learned to drive pretty quickly, even though I was scared.

When my father arrived from Mexico, I got him a job at Foster Farms where I worked. I remember the day that he started work. He didn't want to ride in the car with me. He was really scared. He went on foot because I had barely learned to drive a few days earlier. And I was really worried because my father didn't know I was pregnant. I had to disappear from Livingston where I lived. People would tear me to pieces. I wouldn't be able to stand it. And then what was my father going to think of me? It was impossible for me to stay.

Well, one day, a woman arrived at my house to sell me Avon products—creams and perfumes. I really believe that she was an angel that God sent to me in the form of a woman. She was very friendly to me. She saw my children and started to talk with them, and she told me that she lived in Delhi. She was an American, but she spoke Spanish very well. She was married to a Mexican man. Well, I bought some cream from her so that she would come back, thinking that she could probably help me with my problem. When she came back with the cream, we became better friends. She told me that she was available whenever I needed somebody to take care of the children and that she could also help me if I ever needed an interpreter. She told me that my children appealed to her so much because she didn't have any of her own. That made me feel like there might be a light to brighten my darkness. But I kept going back to the same idea—what about my father? Luckily my father didn't like California. He missed his homeland, Mexico. After three months, he went back to Mexico. Then I could breathe more easily.

A Big Decision

When I was five months pregnant, I had to make a decision. I turned in my resignation at work. I talked to Maria, the woman who sold Avon. She understood my dreadful situation and promised to help me. She was going to take me to Sacramento to look for work in a restaurant. I had only two weeks before I had to leave the chicken plant. I did it without saying anything to anybody about leaving the job. I only told the people in the office. Then I wrote a letter to the guy who was the father of the baby, and my friend took it to him. I told him what was going on, but I never got an answer from him and I never saw him again. Maria took me to Sacramento. I was lucky and got a job in a Mexican restaurant, and they agreed to get in touch with me in a week. I had never worked in a restaurant, but I told them that I had experience working as a waitress in Mexico. I told them I knew it was different here but that they only had to tell me what to do and I could do it.

Maria was ready when they called me to work. She was going to take care of the children. It was so hard for me to leave the children! It felt like death, and all because I couldn't stand people gossiping about me. I wonder why people can't just live their own lives and leave others in peace. Why do they criticize a single mother so much?

Not all of us women have the luck of finding a good man to love us. Why don't people think about how women need men and men need women? There are a lot of single mothers who kill themselves working day and night to support their children and give them an

42

education. They aren't all supported by the government. I know a lot of married couples who get along well and are very happy. But there are other couples who can't stand each other but stay together just so people won't talk about them. How is so much cruelty possible? I had to leave my children for more than two months only because I was going to have a baby with no father around. That's not fair. I had to flee as if I had killed somebody; was anybody going to support me and my children?

One afternoon, they called from Sacramento to tell me that I could start work, and that same night, I turned over my house to the owner. I left without telling anybody, without even saying goodbye to the neighbor who was so good to me, because I didn't want her to ask questions about why I was leaving. Besides, it made me feel very ashamed to talk about my situation.

Like a Criminal

I disappeared during the night like a criminal. I left my children crying—something I will never forget. They didn't want to stay there without their mother. I cried all the way to Sacramento, California, crying and driving. That's not fair. No matter how good or bad we are, we're all human beings, not animals. You might be asking, "Why didn't she take her children?" I didn't have anywhere to live, and I didn't have a cent to rent an apartment. I wanted them with me, but I knew they would be safer with Maria for a while.

Finally, I got to the place. The restaurant where I was going to work is on Twelfth Street in Sacramento. I arrived, tearful, and to tell the truth, I had never worked in a restaurant. I prayed to God with all my heart that He would give me the intelligence I needed for that kind of work. I didn't know how to add or figure out the checks. Do you know how I figured out the checks? I wrote the numbers down and added them up mentally and then wrote the amount. Nobody realized that I didn't know how to do arithmetic. The first night, I told the cook that I didn't know anybody there and I asked her if she could tell me where I could get an inexpensive hotel room, although I really didn't have any money. Then she said I could stay in her apartment because she had an empty room. She said that her husband was a real drunk but that I shouldn't pay attention to him because he didn't cause any problems. She said I could lock my door.

I was glad to accept her offer because I didn't have anywhere to sleep. But what a mess! Her husband didn't let me sleep all night. He shouted at his wife to open the door, that he was going to kill her, and he swore constantly. I spent the night praying out of pure terror. The next day, I told the cook I was very afraid her husband was going to hurt her. I asked if she would do me the favor of letting me sleep in her parking space. I said that I would appreciate it very much and asked her to please not tell anybody I was sleeping in my car.

My Car House

So that's the way it was. I slept in the car for six weeks. I only went into the apartment to bathe and change my clothes. After six weeks, the woman who owned the business said, "I see you're getting a little fatter."

She also asked me how I could live in the cook's apartment with that drunken husband of hers. Then I told her the whole truth about my situation. She was a very good person! They called her La Pelona because she kept her hair very short. When I told her everything, she said, "You're not going to sleep in the car. You'll come to my house until you bring your children here. I'm going to ask a friend of mine to take you to get government aid."

I told her that I had gone to seek government aid and that they had denied it to me. She asked, "Did they know that you were going to have a baby?"

I said that they didn't. Then she said, "They have to help you. Why shouldn't they?"

She took me to live at her house. La Pelona was a very good woman. She had a married son who was separated from his wife because they had marital problems. His wife left him and went back to her family, but when she found out that I was living in her mother-in-law's house where her husband was, she got very jealous and went looking for me at the restaurant. And she said, "Look out because La

44

Pelona's son is my husband and I still love him. Don't go out with him. He flirts a lot."

And I answered, "Don't worry. I don't like married men."

Well, everything worked out for the best, and La Pelona's son reunited with his wife. La Pelona said to me, "How great that she got jealous of you! That made her go back to my son!" Besides, they had a daughter. Well, there I was, living in La Pelona's house. I helped her clean the house when I got home from work. Later her friend took me to the welfare department. After asking me a lot of questions, they gave me aid and a medical card. I hadn't been to see a doctor since I found out I was pregnant. Later on, the same woman came with me to look at a lot of apartment buildings, searching for an apartment to rent, and they all said they didn't want children. We spent two days looking, and we didn't find anything. So back I went to the government office to tell them I had gone to all the apartment buildings and that none of them would take children. Then they found me one and they gave me money so that I could have the kids with me. That was a great relief for my soul because I had been going to see my kids every weekend in Delhi where they were being cared for, and every time I left them, they were crying. I also cried all the way from Delhi back to Sacramento.

A Great Joy

When I had my children with me, I registered them in school and I kept on working until I left work to go to the hospital to have my son, Javier. There was a couple who had a little girl. The husband was Filipino and the wife was Mexican. When she had the little girl, something happened, and she couldn't have any more children. The two of them begged me to give them my baby. They said they would take care of it and love it a lot, and besides, I had three others and I didn't have the money to give them a good education. They said they were financially secure and my son's future would be assured. He'd be in a good school and have a good home with a father and a mother. The idea of giving up my son filled me with terror. How could I give my son up for adoption? They begged me a lot and asked why I wanted more children without a father. But I didn't want to give up my child. How could I make such a brutal decision if my children mean the world to me? That couple got mad at me when they arrived at the hospital, ready for me to hand over my baby. They had brought clothes and even a baby carrier with them, begging me to give them the child. When I refused, they got furious and never talked to me again. How was I going to do that? Impossible!

A Promise

I told myself, "My children are going to study and have professions, even if I have to kill myself working night and day."

And that's the way it was. Nine days after having my baby, I started back to work. How could I live on the money the government gave me when it was hardly enough to pay the rent and the light and gas bills for the apartment? I had no money left to buy food, so instead of one job, I had to have two. I got a part-time job in another place. With that money, I could pay for babysitting and have money to buy food.

But in Sacramento, there were also men looking for easy women, and I had several problems with men who chased after me. It even seemed to me as if I had a sign on my forehead saying, "I'm looking for a man." I guess that's because of my personality. I'm very friendly with people. I think that's why they confused me with an easy woman. I remember what happened to me at the part-time job. I worked at night, Thursday through Sunday. And one Saturday, when I left work, a man began to follow me. And because of trying to lose the man, I got lost. That's because I wasn't familiar with the whole city and I couldn't find Twelfth Street, which was the one that would take me to the street where I lived. Well, I was crying and driving; I was really afraid of stopping and calling anyone on the phone in case the man was still following me. That night, I decided that I had to go back to Foster Farms or get a different job because all the men I met at my other jobs seemed to think I was a worthless piece of garbage.

It seems to me that men fooled around more then than they do now. I remember that in the two restaurants where I worked, they served liquor and the men got really drunk. And when I would go to the table to wait on them, they acted like animals. Excuse the bad comparison! They would try to grab me. They wanted to embrace or kiss me. So one day, I talked to the owner and told her that I was sorry but that I couldn't stand the men who went to that place. I don't know why they were such pests, but the actions made me plan to go back to Turlock, California, and see if I could find work. The woman got very upset. She said, "No, please don't go. I'll raise your salary. Besides, the cook is sick, and if I don't have a cook, I can't open the restaurant."

The owner was such a good person that it was impossible to refuse. I said, "Don't worry. I know how to cook."

And she said to me, "You know how to cook?'

I said, "Of course! I always cook at my house. Besides, the food that's made here isn't a lot of work. Almost everything is prepared in advance."

With a Lot of Love

I cooked for a month, more or less. And that's where I got the idea of one day opening a restaurant. But if I did it, it would be with a lot of love. There were only a few people working in the restaurant, including a man named Raymundo. We were friends, and he was a bachelor. He always told me, "Lupe, you're very young. You need a man so that other men will respect you. And how are you going to make it alone with four kids? Tell me! You need a man to help you. Look, Lupe, I'll really marry you and recognize Javier as my son, and that way everybody will respect you. I promise you I'll love your children a lot, all of them, and I'll treat them with respect." He added, "Think about it. I'm all alone. I don't have anybody here in California."

And I thought, *Well, I guess that would be the best idea because I only expect criticism from my relatives. The farther away, the better.*

I decided to get to know him better before marrying him. It was too soon for me to get married again, since my first marriage had not gone well.

Then I called Maria on the phone. She was like my guardian angel. I told her I was thinking of returning to Delhi and asked if she knew of a house for rent. She said she would look around for me. Then one day, when I didn't have to work, I went to Delhi and I went to a chicken plant in Turlock named Valley Fresh to see if they were taking applications, and there I met the supervisor that I had in Foster Farms in Livingston. I asked if he had work for me, and he answered, "When do you want to start?"

I said, "As soon as I can. I have to move here from Sacramento."

And he said, "Call me as soon as you're ready."

So then I went to see Maria, and she had found a house for me to rent. We went to see it and we spoke to the owners, and they said that they would rent me the house. That made me very happy. But I didn't know what to say to the owner of the restaurant in Sacramento, especially since she didn't want me to leave the job. Well, I had to tell her, even though it made me feel bad because she had been very good to me. When I went to return the keys to her, I said that I was very sorry but that I was giving back the keys. Besides, the cook was well now. She didn't want to accept the keys. She said, "I don't want you to go."

I said to her, "Please. I have to go."

She still refused the keys, and I had to take them with me.

That was in November of 1967, and my friend helped to move the few things I had. I didn't even say goodbye to La Pelona. But it was impossible for me to stay. She only paid me $1.65 an hour, and that wasn't much. And besides, the poor thing couldn't pay more. I began to work in the Turlock plant. And then I got work for my friend Raymundo, but he didn't have a car to get to work. So he came to live in our house with us. Well, the work seemed very hard to him. Although he was a good person and affectionate with my children, his customs were very different from mine. He spent whatever little money he earned with his friends, and he always asked me to lend him the car. Whenever I needed the car to do my errands, he would be off somewhere else. That's how five months passed until one day, he left work and went to the office to quit without telling me anything. Then the supervisor came over to where I was working and said, "Lupe, your friend quit and left."

And I said, "What do you mean he quit?"

(Left to right) Esmeralda, Gloria, Lupe, Javier, Rafael, 1968

He just said, "Yes."

That same day, I said to myself, *Lupe, you are the most stupid woman on earth. Are you going to work to support a lazy bum just so that other women will respect you? And besides, he's using your car to go partying!*

I had also heard that he had been seen with a woman in my car in the park. I thought, *Why am I so foolish?*

Now I really felt desperate. I was living in Delhi and working in Turlock. Along the road, I talked to myself and cried buckets. I asked myself, *How could I have gone to live in Sacramento just because I didn't want people to know I was going to have a baby with no father in sight? Now what am I going to do? Now they'll really have something to talk about!*

Then I thought, *Let them talk until they get tired. At any rate, nobody's going to support me.*

When I got to the house, my friend Raymundo wasn't there. I was furious with him and with myself. When he got there, I was ready and waiting for him. I said to him immediately, "Why did you leave the job?"

He answered, "That's a lousy job. I'm not going to work there anymore."

I said, "Okay. That's your problem. But you're not going to live in my house."

He answered, "But why should I leave? I can get another job."

And I said, "Why? To spend everything you earn on your friends? It'll be better once and for all if you go someplace else."

And he, at least, understood that what he was doing wasn't right, and he went to Texas to be with some friends. That experience bothered me a lot and did me a lot of damage. I felt defeated inside, but I still had hopes of finding a good man; however, one has never arrived.

A Dream Come True

So instead of being destroyed, I kept on fighting. I wanted to buy a house. I didn't want to pay rent my whole life. I thought, *I have to buy a house for my children.*

I couldn't forget that in Sacramento, it had been really difficult for me to rent an apartment. Wherever I went, they wouldn't accept children, and that made me furious. I worked really hard in 1968. Every weekend of that summer, I worked in the fields. When there was no work in the plant, I went with my friends to pick tomatoes, chili peppers, and strawberries. I was also working in a fast food place that sold tacos. Well, when I had saved one thousand dollars in the bank, I said, "I'm going to look for a house to buy."

I went to see my friend Maria, the one who sold Avon products, and I told her I wanted to buy a house. She said, "Lupe, do you really have the money?"

I answered, "Yes, I have one thousand dollars."

And she answered, "How do you think you can buy a house with a thousand dollars?"

I said, "Let's go ask."

It was a Thursday in January 1969, and a block away from where I lived, there was a house with a sign out front saying it was for sale and that the owner would finance it. It seemed like a palace to me. I said to Maria, "Look at that house. Let's go ask."

Then she said, "Let's."

We went to see the owner, and he was very pleasant to us. He asked me some questions, such as where I was renting and where I worked. And I told him I had only one thousand dollars for a down payment. He told me the house would cost $11,000 and that he would accept my thousand-dollar down payment. I almost cried from happiness. And the good man said to me, "Tomorrow I'll check on your employment, and if everything is in order, you can move into the house this weekend."

He showed me the inside of the house, and I took the children in with me. They were really happy.

Another friend said to me that if she, who spoke good English, had been taken for a fool when she and her husband bought their house, what were they going to do to me?

I said, "Well, I'll wait and see."

The next Friday, when I got home from work, the babysitter told me that the man who was selling the house had come to look for me and that I should call him as soon as I arrived. I called him, and he said, "Lupe, everything is okay. On Monday, you can give me the down payment, the thousand dollars, and we'll go to the lawyer and sign all the papers. You can move in whenever you want. Come and get the key."

That same weekend, some of my friends helped me move the few things I had. Everything I had was secondhand. And what do you suppose happened that same weekend? Sunday afternoon, I went to Livingston to wash my clothes. On the way home, I had an accident, and my car was totaled. The ambulance took me and the other family, a woman with her children, to the hospital. She was the one at fault. Then the police went to my house to say that I had

had an accident, and all of children were crying, thinking I was dead. But thank God, I only had bruises and a few slightly broken teeth. Then the man I was buying the house from came to see me, and I asked if he would do me the favor of waiting until I could get up and go to the bank to take out the money for him. And the man said to me, "Lupe, just give me five hundred dollars and keep the other five hundred to buy yourself another car."

My car had been totaled; if he hadn't been so kind, how would I have gotten to work? Can you believe that in this world, there are bad people, but there are also many good people? That man was American. He didn't know me, and I didn't know him. But that's the way I bought my first house.

Wanting to Prosper

From 1969 to 1971, I worked in the plant and also in the fields in the summers. On weekends, I worked in Turlock in a restaurant that specialized in Mexican food. There was also a bar. Sometimes the owner would have me work in the bar, taking drinks to the tables. That's where I really learned about purgatory. The drunks were so obnoxious they made me cry. One day, a man said to me, "If you're so decent, why do you work here?"

To make me feel better, the owner of the place said, "Don't pay any attention to them. You shouldn't cry. Think of it as job like any other job. Don't let what they say bother you."

I worked three nights: Friday, Saturday, and Sunday. Every Monday, I went to work at the plant without sleeping. It was very hard; I remember very well. One night, I left work at 2:00 a.m. and I opened the door of my car and saw a man inside. I almost fainted. I ran and knocked on the door of the owner of the restaurant and said, "There's a man inside my car!"

And she called the police, and they took him out. But by then, I was very afraid of working there. At the same time, I couldn't really quit because I had a plan to save my money to start my own taco shop. I was saving all my tips and part of what they were paying me there.

CHAPTER 3

Happiness and Disaster

An Impossible Love

ABOUT EIGHTEEN MONTHS AFTER MY friend Raymundo left the house, I met a single man named Gonzalo, and I began to go out with him. We became very good friends. Then it was love! The kind of love that kills you and doesn't let you see beyond your own nose! At that time, I stopped working at the Mexican restaurant. Gonzalo told me that I should stop working there and that he would help me out with money. He was very decent and hardworking, without bad habits. He treated my children very well, but he never spoke of marrying me. I always washed his clothes and I made his food—everything that a wife does. But he sent all the money he earned to his parents. Well, it wasn't important to me for the first three years.

I had saved five thousand dollars by then, and I had the idea of looking for a place to open a taco shop. I made the decision and went to see Olivia, a woman who worked in real estate, and I told her what I wanted. She said she would look for a place for me. A week later, she called me on the phone and said that she found a place and that I should go talk to the owner. And that's the way it was. We got together with the owner, and I asked him if five thousand dollars would be enough to fix up the place and buy the equipment. He told me that yes, it was enough. He offered to help me himself. He said he had a carpenter that didn't charge much, so right away we began to put in the kitchen and the plumbing. It took about three months to get it done. I never thought so many things would be needed to open a restaurant. When I went to take the money out of the bank to pay for all the work, the manager said to me, "Lupe, you don't know what you are doing. What do you mean you're going to open a restaurant?"

I answered, "That's the way it is."

"But do you know how to cook?" he asked me.

I said that I did. He said, "But, Lupe, you're very young. You don't know how to speak English. How do you think you're going to do it?"

He also told me that ninety percent of new businesses fail and that I ought to realize I was throwing my money away. That it was a lot of sacrifice to save five thousand dollars only to lose them in the business I wanted to start. At that time, I had a medical card for myself and my children. So a social worker came to my house to give me advice about what it meant to have a business. She said I had no experience and that I shouldn't open that business, that it would be better to just forget it. And I answered that I had signed the contract and that if I failed, I would go back to the chicken plant. And the woman just shook her head. But when I paid for all the work that had been done in the place, I got a big surprise. The five thousand dollars was hardly enough to pay for the work that had been done on the building. I didn't have enough then for the pots and pans, tables, and chairs. That's when the good stuff began.

I thought I had credit at one bank and two finance companies. So there I went with my daughter Gloria, who was the interpreter. Well, they all shut the door in my face. Money to start a business? they said, nothing doing. That ninety percent went bankrupt. They asked where my brain was since I had no experience. I told them I would put my house up as collateral. But nothing worked for me. Well, I already had a name for the restaurant—La Morenita. When I thought of the name, I was thinking of the Dark Virgin of Guadalupe. The people I worked with were already laughing at me, saying that I was crazy. They said I was only dreaming. But I laughed right with them and didn't pay any attention. But when I couldn't get the money that I needed—five thousand dollars more—I was really sad, crying and thinking that what everybody had told me was true and that I was going to lose my money. I just begged God to open a door for me.

Well, there was an American lady, Christine, who took my children to church every Sunday because I always worked Sundays. She picked them up at home. And one of those Sundays, the priest said in church that if anybody knew of a person in need, to ask that everybody pray for that person. Then my daughter Gloria said that her mother was going to open a restaurant but couldn't now because she still needed five thousand dollars that she hadn't been able to get. She said her mother was very sad, crying at home, and she asked everybody to pray for her. And at that moment, Christine, that wonderful woman, said that she would lend me the money that I needed. I'll never forget the joy it gave me to know that woman believed in me. My children hugged me happily when they got home. And for the rest of my life, I'm going to be grateful to that woman. I still remember how I made the menus and covered them in plastic sleeves with logos that the Pepsi company gave me. I did the whole menu in Spanish. Now when I remember how I did everything when I started the business, it really makes me laugh. A lot of people really helped me!

(Left to right) Lupe, Esmeralda, Gloria, Javier, Rafael, 1972

The Great Moment

I remember the first day we opened the restaurant to practice a little for four hours, from about 6:00 to 10:00 p.m. How can I forget that day? We had told all the friends we had we were going to open the restaurant. I thought that if I could sell $50 worth of food each day, in six days it would be three hundred dollars. That seemed like a lot to me. In the plant, the most I could earn if I worked six days was between $85 and $90.

Well, those first four hours when we opened the restaurant were pure joy. I was the only cook! The waitress was my friend Sara, and my children were there, celebrating. Everyone was very happy, running around everywhere. And what was the big surprise? Well, in the first four hours we were open, we sold $80 worth of food. That really seemed like a lot to me. We were all just about dying from joy, but what I was doing was incredible. When they brought me the orders, I sliced the meat and I cut the lettuce and the tomatoes. And when they asked for sopes, I also made them. I didn't have anything prepared in advance, except for rice, beans, green and red chili, and the salsa for the enchiladas. I made everything else when they ordered it.

So I was all alone with only one helper, the waitress. My children were little, but the oldest, Gloria, was thirteen years old and she helped me on the weekends. The first six months were really hard. We had a lot of customers. Some came just out of curiosity. I thought that I had survived in the plant for about eight years, but I wouldn't last even a year in the restaurant. The hardest thing was not being able to be with my children at home. Sometimes the youngest would call me up, crying that he was hungry and that nobody was feeding him. That hurt me a lot.

Also, in that first year, Javier, the youngest, nearly burned the house down. The only thing that saved it was that I had a smoke alarm. The neighbors heard it, and they ran over to put out the fire. It really worried me to just think about what would have happened if my son had burned himself. A niece named Socorro took care of Javier for me. She called me up, so frightened that she could hardly talk. She said, "Auntie, the house is burning."

And the only thing I said to her was, "Get out of the house," and I ran out of the restaurant.

A customer took me home. When I got to Delhi, there were a lot of people outside the house. The firemen were getting rid of the smoke because my neighbor Larry had already put out the fire. And there was Javier, very frightened, pale, and trembling. But that child was really something else. He was seven years old when he did that. I had a can of gasoline for the lawn mower, and he had gotten hold of the can and poured gasoline in the garage. He told me that he lit a match and when he saw the flame, he grabbed the hose and tried to put the fire out. But that just made more flames, and he didn't know what to do. Then the alarm went off, and fortunately for us, the neighbor was home. He ran over and put the fire out.

Afterward, Javier begged me to buy him a bicycle. He said, "Mommy, I want a bicycle!"

He pestered me so much that I finally bought it for him. I told him that he had to understand that he couldn't go very far away on his bike, that he could just go to school. It was close by, just two blocks away. He said, "Yes, Mommy."

Well, just imagine how surprised I was when one day he came to the restaurant on his bike, all sunburned. It was almost ten miles from the house to the restaurant, and he had gone on Highway 99. I almost died from the shock. A seven-year-old child riding his bike on the freeway! And how come not even one police officer saw him? Well, the next day, he didn't have a bicycle anymore. We took off the tires so he couldn't use it.

Oh, Lord! When Rafael and Javier were little boys, they were really something else! They just loved dogs. Well, they wanted a dog so much that somebody gave them one, and they named it Blackie. That dog really made me mad. When he got bigger, he did a lot of damage in my garden. I've loved flowers all my life, and that dog always dug holes around the plants, and sometimes he even dug them up and broke them. Well, I couldn't stand it. Even though my children adored him, one day, I put him in the car and I took him far away with the idea of leaving him to get lost. I took him out of the car and said, "You stay here. You're too mischievous with my plants."

And when he looked at me so sadly because I was going to leave him, it made me very sad. Well, I couldn't leave him. I went back and picked him up and took him home. I often remember that dog. One time I went on vacation to Mexico with all the children for two weeks, and we left the dog with our neighbor. When we came back, the dog was so happy to see us that he came for a hug from each one of us. I was really surprised when I saw what he did. Now I think that a dog is a family's best friend.

At that time, we closed the restaurant every Monday, so that was the day I could spend with my children. When they had vacation time, we would go to parks or other places they liked. And that's how the years from 1972 to 1974 passed.

By then, I was thinking that my daughters were twelve and fifteen years old, respectively. And I was setting a bad example for them living with a man I wasn't married to. That wasn't what my parents had taught me, so I made a decision that, like many others, cost me a lot of pain and tears. I decided to say something to the man with whom I had shared my private life for four years. I got my courage together and one day I told him that if he really loved me, he should marry me and work to support me and my children and that we should become a real family, because I had always been the one who had all the responsibility for the house, my family, and my children. He sent all the money he made to his parents in Mexico, and I wasn't willing to go on the same way. Can you believe what he told me? After four years of living with me as if I were his wife, he said, "How can you think that I would marry a woman who's had another man's children? Do you think I want to have children with a woman who has another man's children? Do you think you deserve to get my check? Where is your brain?"

Well, that answer broke my heart into a thousand pieces. In that instant, I told him to get out of my house and said that I would never go back to him even if I died from sadness. So he left the house. And I was alone again with only my children. I cried a lot over that, especially because my youngest son loved him very much. But what could I expect from that man? Absolutely nothing. In four years, he had only given me a pair of shoes and a hundred and fifty dollars to buy a stereo set, and I ended up paying for that. Later he asked me a lot of times to get back together with him, but he had already broken my heart. I had lost all the faith and trust I had in him. And to top things off, one day, he went to my business and fought with one of my employees. That hurt me so much. He made a laughingstock of me in front of my employees and the customers in the restaurant. That was the end. I even had to call the police. I didn't want them to throw him in jail; I only wanted him to quit bothering me.

The restaurant I had in Turlock was very small, with only seven tables. Everything was very crowded. One day, the owner of the building came to the restaurant and told me he had a business site available in Livingston. He told me that it was bigger than my restaurant and close to Highway 99 and that I should go see it and he would let me have it if I wanted it. So I went to see the place. It was in bad shape, but the owner would help me out if I would take it. Well, I thought it was a good thing for me, and we made a deal.

Love Grows

I got the place fixed up, and we made it look cleaner. I now had some people to leave in charge of the Turlock business, and it didn't cost me a lot of money to open the new place. I had the two businesses for one year, but it was very hard for me. Besides, I was always teaching people how to cook. As soon as they learned, they left the job. There was a woman who was very interested in buying the Turlock restaurant. I decided to sell it to her and to just keep the one in Livingston because it was much bigger. With the money from the sale, I remodeled the whole place. I put in new booths and tables and new curtains in the dining room and part of the kitchen. I put in some plants and flowers.

That was in 1976, and I was living in Delhi. I was thinking about selling my house and buying one in Turlock, because there were no houses across the street from where I was living. There were only nut orchards. I got home from work very late, after midnight, and I was a little afraid. I wondered if a robber would be hiding behind the trees when I got home. So a few months later, I went to look for a real estate agent and I said that I wanted to sell my house. That was in September of 1976. They went to see how much the house was worth, and it turns out that the house was worth more than twice what I paid for it! In November, they put up the "FOR SALE" sign.

Who would have thought that in one week there would be a buyer for the house? I still hadn't gone to look for another house! Well, my children and I went to look at houses. We didn't find one that we liked, and the man who wanted our house wanted to move in quickly. We kept looking until we found one that didn't cost too much and wasn't in the downtown area of the city, because I don't like to live downtown. That house was much prettier than our other one. It had better architecture. We were very excited. It cost us $37,500, and we moved in on March 7, 1977. I used part of the extra money from the sale of the house to buy new furniture and saved the rest. The new house already was carpeted. Each year that passed, my dreams were becoming a reality not only because of a lot of work but also because of a lot of love.

Esmeralda's Fifteenth Birthday

I remember Esmeralda's fifteenth birthday. She said to me, "Mom, I want you to have a quinceañera for me. I want to have ladies-in-waiting with their escorts."

And I said to her, "Oh, honey, I don't have time to arrange for all of that. I'm working too hard. A quinceañera takes as much work as a wedding!"

But she wanted the party and she said, "I'll arrange everything. I'll get all the young people who'll be my attendants. You just have to make the food and pay for a musical group to play for four hours so we can celebrate and dance. And if you want, I'll take care of the invitations and getting the place. Mom, I'm never going to be fifteen years old again. Don't worry, Mom. All the girls pay for their own dresses, and the boys pay for their suits. You don't have to spend too much money."

Well, as usual, I couldn't deny anything to my child. The first thing I thought was, *If I don't give them what they want, who will? They don't have a father.*

She took charge of all the arrangements. She was quite chubby, so she went on a strict diet. On her birthday, she was really slender. She got the invitations, the place, and some police officers to keep order during the dance. And I made the meal for all the guests, and there were a lot of them, counting our many friends and the families that came with them. One thing I can say is that even if I didn't have enough money, I would go so far as to borrow it in order to give my children what they wanted. They meant everything to me, and I worked hard to provide for them.

Running the Business

Now my whole family works in our restaurants, even two of my oldest granddaughters. I've worked hard to keep a good reputation for the business and the food because anybody can open a business, but keeping it going for so many years is what is hard. One really has to take all the responsibility no matter how much help or how many employees there are. Money is a very strange thing. If you don't take care of it or know how to manage it, it gets spent very easily, and then there's not even enough left to pay for the basic business expenses.

An inspector gave me some advice when I started the business. He said that if I wanted to get ahead, I would have to watch the pennies. Do you know why he said that? Because if we don't take care of the little things, it's very hard to get ahead. Lots of people don't pay attention to the little things; they're just as important as the big ones, whether you believe it or not. Let's say that an employee marks his time card five minutes earlier that he really arrives each day. Just figure out how much could be lost on just one person in a month! Now think about all the little things that have to be taken care of in any business. To say it another way, a person can keep buying clothes and shoes, but if that person doesn't take care of them, I'm sure she or he will never have anything presentable to wear.

I remember that when I started the business, people would often ask me, "Lupe, what do you put in the food to make it so good?" And I would answer, "I put in a lot of love."

But my life was full of laughter and tears.

Gloria, Esmeralda

Esmeralda's Wedding

Barely a year after her fifteenth birthday, on June 30, 1978, Esmeralda married Jorge Delgado. She never really gave me any problems. She was a good kid, and I already knew that she had a boyfriend. They had been going together for four years, beginning when she was twelve years old. I guess it's because by age eleven, she already developed into a young woman. Sometimes they broke up and then they got back together again. He was the first boyfriend she had. He came to my house every day, and when we went out somewhere, he almost always came with us. I looked on him as another son. Well, one day, Esmeralda told me they were getting married, and I said, "What do you mean you're getting married?"

She hadn't even finished high school. She told me that she didn't like school very much and that probably she would finish her studies later. Well, I tried to give her advice about marriage. I told her to look at what was happening to me, although not all men are alike. Still, she didn't want to wait any longer, so what could I do? Well, give her a wedding! And she didn't want just any wedding—she wanted a big wedding with a lot of bridesmaids, ushers, and godparents. Then I thought, since I didn't have the pleasure of getting married with a beautiful long lace dress, my daughters can get married the way they want to and with all the luxuries that we can afford.

Esmeralda and husband George

Well, thank God, her wedding was everything she wanted, including a beautiful dress. On the day of her wedding, I said that I wasn't going to cry because that brought bad luck, and besides, I was getting another son. He's a very good person with no bad habits. But I scolded Esmeralda for something else before leaving the church on her wedding day. That was because she went to a beauty parlor to have her hair done and she got home late, and to top everything off, there was no gasoline in the car we were using to get to the church. We had to get gas with her in her wedding gown because we were out of time, and everybody was looking, as if to say, "What's going on with that bride?"

She looked as beautiful as a queen. She got married just as I dreamed, leaving my house dressed in white. I prayed that she wouldn't have the same bad luck I had. I always prayed to God to take care of my daughters because what was happening to me was not at all pleasant, and I didn't want the same thing to happen to them for anything in the world.

Disaster in Livingston

One day in September of 1978, at about one in the afternoon, when the restaurant was full of people because it was the lunch hour, a huge semitruck came down the street, and what do you think happened? All the electric wires of the restaurant exploded, and so did the fuse box. The explosion was so powerful that it was just like a bolt of lightning. You could see flames everywhere. Everybody ran out, frightened, and there was really a lot of damage. We had to close the business for more than eight weeks.

Since this accident happened on a Friday, I had a lot of meat and vegetables and tortillas in the walk-in cooler. I had a lot of merchandise on hand, and the worst of it was that I didn't have insurance to cover the time when I couldn't work. Only the merchandise and the equipment were insured. That experience really taught me a lesson. Afterward, I got a good insurance policy in case of another accident. When they finally fixed the electric wires, we reopened the business and moved on. But I never imagined what was waiting for me down the road.

Well, that year went by, and in November of 1979, I was told that they were going to auction off the apartment property that was behind my business. A lawyer friend of mine said they were going to auction it off through the court and that if I were interested, he could go as my representative. He would only need $10,000. He said that it would be good for me since it was right next to my business. Well, I didn't have that much money because the extra money from the house I sold had been used as the down payment on some duplexes that I had bought in Turlock. Then I told my cousin Manuel Valencia about the property they were going to auction off, and he said that if I wanted to try to get the property, he would lend me the money I needed. So the lawyer went to represent me. Four other people were also going to take part in the court auction.

Investment

It turned out that nobody else in court had the $10,000 for the down payment, so I got the property. Well, the apartments were very old. Just two months after I bought them, some authorities from the city of Livingston came to the restaurant and brought me an order to fix up the apartments and paint and repair certain things. At that time, two young men came by to ask me for work painting. They said they knew how to repair buildings and houses. Somebody gave me references on them, and so I contracted them to do all of the work on the apartments and some things on my house. We became very good friends. Because they were working for me, I always let them eat at the restaurant at no charge.

But then I had been drinking every day for about a year. I didn't go and drink in bars. I did it at home and at the restaurant, hiding from my children. When they found the bottles hidden here and there, they said, "Mom, please don't drink. That's not good, Mom."

I was drinking strong whiskey with soda because I was feeling very disillusioned about men. There was a cook named Jose who worked for me. According to him, he loved me so much he was dying over me. He even went to talk to the priest at church to tell him that I didn't believe that he loved me. Can you believe it? According to him, he wanted to marry me immediately. Well, I was beginning to think it was true.

And one day, two girls that always came to the restaurant arrived. Sometimes they ate there and sometimes they got food to go. One time, Jose waited on them and served them their food. I was waitressing that day. Although I didn't know it, one of them was his girlfriend. Somehow it occurred to me to open their bag of food to go before charging them for it. I saw a handful of roses next to the plates, and the roses were from the garden I had behind the restaurant. And do you know what I did with the roses? I threw them in the cook's face! Afterward, I told him what a liar he was. And he left the job; he quit. Actually, that was the best thing that could happen. So with all the things that were happening to me and all the responsibility of my business, my house, my children, their studies, and to top it off, heartless men playing with my feelings, I began to drink hard liquor.

CHAPTER 4

Second Marriage

The Beginning of a Disastrous Ending

AROUND THAT TIME, AURORA BARRON, a daughter of my sister Alvina, came from Mexico to live with me. She worked as a cook in my business and was a very good worker. I also had a very good waitress, who was just like a member of the family. When my niece Aurora's birthday arrived, I wanted to have a little party and some birthday cake for her. So that day, after closing the restaurant, I invited a group of friends and I also invited the painters who had painted the apartments for me. One of them talked a lot with me that day about loneliness and many other things. I told him how I had arrived in California. I also told him that with the help of God, I was going to achieve everything I wanted, even if I killed myself working day and night. He also told me about his family and said that he had no immigration papers; they were all illegal aliens. That's the day that marked the beginning of a great story that would last for eleven years filled with a lot of love, hopes, and passions. But that ended in complete disaster.

Love Frequently Brings Pain

I don't know how he did it, but that man succeeded in stealing my heart. In spite of the fact that he was fifteen years younger than me and that I didn't have any faith in him, he got what he wanted. I wasn't a child. My daughter Esmeralda was already married, Gloria was at the university, Rafael was in high school, and Javier was in junior high.

My children and I had many decent friendships. I don't understand how I could have allowed myself to be so foolish as to accept that man's advances. Several times, in groups of four to six people, we went out to dance or to the park or sometimes to Reno, Nevada. At that time, I was still drinking, even though I often did it secretly. One time, I went out with the painter and we had sex. Afterward, I was very, very sorry. But I said to myself, the only person that I'm hurting is myself.

What I didn't think was that I was going to get pregnant immediately. Then I told him, but what can you expect of a man that's just twenty-one years old? He told me, "Go get an abortion."

I told him that after I had done so many dumb things to myself, I wasn't going to commit a crime. I told him to get out of my life and that I was never going to say who my baby's father was. But unfortunately, we kept seeing each other. I knew he didn't love me and that for him it was just sex and that for me he was just a friend. Well, my dear readers, you can just imagine what was waiting for me from my family, my children, and my other relatives. But I already loved my baby, and at that moment, the pain and suffering didn't seem important. That took place in 1980. It's been seventeen years since that happened, but whenever I remember those moments, it still makes me cry. How can I forget it? When my oldest son realized what was happening, he said to me, "Aren't you tired of bringing up kids without a father? And now you're going to have another one!"

When Gloria, who was studying at the university in Santa Cruz, came home during her vacation, she didn't want to come to my house, even though I was paying all her expenses. She didn't want to talk to me. I think the whole thing made her feel ashamed when she was with her friends. Sometimes when she had a vacation, she went to a friend's house instead of mine. The only ones who never said anything negative to me were Esmeralda and Javier.

Life and Destruction

As if all this weren't enough, on July 20 of the same year, 1980, my restaurant burned down completely. There were only ashes left. That was on a Monday. I had gone to the movies with some friends and, of course, the painter. But I want you to know that he didn't live at my house. Well, my cousin Manuel called the house to tell me that the restaurant was burning, and they told him that I was at the movies. So he called the theater. When they gave me the news, I couldn't speak. My legs didn't want to move. My whole body was trembling. I had to sit down for several minutes. I had insurance but I still felt a terrible pain inside of me. I don't think that anybody else could understand it. My heart was aching, and I felt as if the world had gotten darker for me. At that moment, I thought I heard a voice saying, "Lupe, you've lost everything."

Eight years of sacrifice had become ashes in a matter of minutes. That's the way it is when there are people who do cruel things for a little money, because that's what happened. At that time, I didn't have the cash on hand because I had invested everything in the apartments. I hope the people who did that terrible thing have truly asked for God's forgiveness. Well, there I went to the insurance company with everything completely burned down. The insurance company asked me questions that went back to before I was born. They dragged me back and forth, and it was all for nothing. The actual owner of the building had died six months earlier. His children didn't want to sign papers, saying that I was the owner of all the restaurant equipment. I could have died, but that wouldn't have accomplished anything. The insurance only paid for the merchandise that I had lost. That was practically nothing. That event almost destroyed me.

But life goes on, so I had to find strength and think about my family. I asked myself how I was going to pay for Gloria's education and the household expenses, especially since I was pregnant. Well, I still got some money from the apartment rents, so at least, I could buy food. I also had some duplexes that I had bought with the extra money from the house I had sold, and I decided to sell them. I told some neighbors who lived next door that I wanted to sell the duplexes. They went to see them and they liked them. They bought them from me and gave me $15,000, which was what I had paid as a down payment. With that, I could pay my outstanding bills. I couldn't count on the father of the baby I was going to have. In fact, he wanted me to pay the bill I still owed him for the repairs to the apartments.

So that's the way it went, in bumps and jerks and with me hiding from my friends. I didn't want anybody to see me. When anybody came to the house, I pretended I wasn't home and didn't open the door. I watered the flowers around the house at night when my unborn baby was well hidden. My neighbor didn't even realize I was pregnant until I had my daughter Erica, who was born on November 14, 1980. She saved me from alcoholism. After I got pregnant with her, I stopped drinking.

When the baby was born, my children knew who the father was. He took me to the hospital and was then with me until she was born. A week later, he went to Mexico. He called me very frequently, and it was almost always a collect call. Then I wrote to his mother and I asked her to give some advice to her son: that he should forget me, that I was too old for him, that besides I already had grown children, that the relationship wasn't good for him or for me, and that he shouldn't see me again. But instead of helping me by giving my advice to her son, the woman answered me and said I shouldn't even think that her son would let his daughter go without a father. She said he was a good person and that he had told her that he really loved me and the baby and that he would soon return from Mexico, only he had no immigration papers. When he came four months later, he got as far as Tijuana, Baja California. He called me and said he was coming to my house. But it turned out that he couldn't cross the border. Every time he tried, the immigration agents would catch him and throw him out of the country. One time, when he tried to cross with the help of a coyote, the immigration agents caught them and threw them in jail for three weeks in San Diego. He called me from there several times, and his mother also called me, begging me to please help her son. She would cry every time she called and asked me what her son would do if I didn't help him. She said he would die of hunger. And because I also had suffered when I got to California, I felt sorry for him, especially since they were also a very poor family in Mexico. But what could I do? He was a prisoner. Well, when they let him go, he tried to cross the border, and they threw him out again. At that time, I had a new car, a Camaro, and he called and said, "Lupe, why don't you come for me in your car? Tell your son-in-law, Jorge, to come with you. I'm sick and I can't cross the border. Besides, I don't have any money."

Charity

Well, I really felt sorry for him. I asked Jorge, my daughter Esmeralda's husband, if the two of them would go with me, and they said yes. We went and we brought him back in April of 1981. He was really sick and very skinny. According to him, he was ready to stay and live with me and his daughter in my house. We talked about the situation a lot, but my children didn't really like the idea. The truth is that it wasn't easy for me either. It was like having another child to care for. He had absolutely nothing. How was he going to help me? He didn't have work, and I didn't either. It was really hard to take on the expenses of seven people. But he kept telling me that he didn't want to leave his daughter and that he and I could work together. He said that he loved his daughter a lot and that he would never interfere with my other children.

Well, I started to think the damage was already done and that we should try it out and see if we could make a life together without getting married. At that time, the woman named Matilde, who had bought the restaurant I sold in Turlock, came to look for me at home to ask if I would like to take care of the business for her for six months because she was very sick and wanted to go to Mexico for treatment. I said, "Back to the place where I started in 1972 all over again?"

But when you've lost everything, what else can you do? I accepted the deal. As I said earlier, it was a very small restaurant with only seven tables, which was why I sold it in the first place. I knew that the woman had lost a lot of clients. She was almost bankrupt. Well, we put a big sign in the window of the restaurant, saying that La Morenita was returning. The first day we opened, we had a line of people waiting for tables, thank God. Although the restaurant was very small, I found a little place in the kitchen to put a cradle for my baby. She was a very good baby. She didn't cry a lot, and I could take care of her while her father washed the dishes. I did the cooking and I had to listen to a lot of personal criticism. I had to take it and pretend I was deaf so that I would not explode like a balloon. Even though I was strong, it wasn't enough for me. Lots of people thought of me as less than garbage. At least, that's the way they made me feel.

Well, about a month after the painter arrived, a brother and a sister of his came, and they expected to stay in my house. The family was growing very fast. It was more responsibility for me. They didn't have any money either. Well, I put the painter's sister to work for me in the restaurant, and his brother stayed home for about two months until he found work and went to live somewhere else. During those six months that I worked in the Turlock restaurant, a friend told me that there was a restaurant in Ceres, California, that was in very bad shape and that the owner was renting it with all its equipment. He didn't have much clientele. We went to see the place and we liked it because it was very big. And the best thing was that we didn't need much money to open it because it had all the necessary equipment. Although the owner was Assyrian and it was a little difficult to negotiate with him, we made the deal for three years. We just wanted to wait for Matilde's return from Mexico at the end of the six months.

Gloria's Wedding

In that same year, on June 20, 1981, my daughter Gloria graduated as a teacher and immediately got married to Marcos Smallwood. Her wedding was very different from Esmeralda's. Marcos is not Catholic; he belongs to a Pentecostal church. They didn't want to have a dance. They only wanted a meal and a toast with cider because nobody drinks alcoholic beverages in that church.

Nevertheless, she got married like a queen, dressed in white and with bridesmaids and groom's men, but the group was much smaller than Esmeralda's wedding party. As they left the church, I surprised them by having a mariachi group playing. They also played during the reception. The bride and groom went from the church to the reception in an antique convertible car. We had lots of guests, and everything was the way they wanted it. Gloria had said to me, "You have to cry, Mom, when I get married. If you don't cry, it's because you don't love me."

But I didn't cry. That's because they had been going together for years, and I knew Marcos's parents very well. They were very good people, and besides, the newlyweds were going to live very close to me. What more could I want for my daughters? Each girl married their first boyfriend. Although they occasionally quarreled and broke up for a while and even went out with others, in the end, they made up and got back together.

Reconciliation

I am sure that Gloria didn't want to share the same house with the painter. When I was going to have my daughter Erica, Gloria was very mad at me. After I gave her a beautiful wedding party with a banquet and a mariachi, which was my responsibility to do, she became more affectionate with the baby. She took her along wherever she went.

Well, the six months passed rapidly. Matilde returned, and I turned the business over to her on the last day of October 1981. There were a lot of customers now, and we had the contract in Ceres to move it, fix up the place, and take out licenses and permits. I was able to borrow the money we needed. We opened on January 1, 1982. Even though we had experience, we still had to have some publicity. It was a new place where not everybody knew us. We put out the La Morenita sign, and the first two days we sold two meals for the price of one. The business started to take off. The painter worked right along with me, and it seemed that everything was going well. I worked every day and double shifts on the weekends.

Gloria and Mark, 1981

A few months later, the painter asked me to send letters inviting his parents to visit us so that they could get tourist visas and come to California. Since he wanted them to come, I said yes and sent them the letters. Because they were elderly, they got lifetime visas. They could come whenever they wanted to.

After his parents came, he began to beg me to marry him. He was worried because I didn't want to get married. Then he began to get jealous of all the men who said hello to me or who talked to me for any reason, even our workers. It hurt me when he said I didn't want to marry him because I wanted to be free and that I only wanted him to help me at work and that when I got tired of him, I would throw him out in the street. He also said that I wanted to go out with other men and that's why I wouldn't marry him. But the truth is that inside of me, I felt that all the love he said he felt for me was a lie. I don't know why but I felt that he wasn't sincere. His family also showed me a lot of love, but inside of me, I felt that wasn't sincere either. I don't know why, but he even cried when I would say that it was a very big decision and that I didn't think I could stand any more disillusionments. And he was very young. One day, he was going to want his freedom, and I didn't feel like I could take it.

But he insisted and insisted, and his family also asked why I wouldn't marry him when he loved me so much. He said that the only important things to him were me and the baby. But I had other things to consider. He had no experience with the business and he wasn't a legal resident in California. And if after marrying him I had to arrange immigration papers for him, what would happen then? But the most stubborn one always wins, so I finally decided to marry him. I spoke to my children, and they said, "Well, if you want to, do it, but make sure it's with separate property."

And I answered, "But I only have the house and the apartments, and I bought them when I didn't even know him. He can never ask me for any part of that."

The Motive behind the Marriage

Well, it seemed silly to me to get married with separate property, but we got married. Our celebration was a toast on October 18, 1982. We were married for barely two months when he demanded that we make the application for immigration papers. We went and turned in the application, and I thought then that he would be calmer. But he just waited a few months and then began to bug me about going to a lawyer to make a contract in case anything happened so that he would get half of whatever we had made or done together. And I asked him, "But why? We're married, and if anything happened, you would get your share."

But he said, "You have other children, and if anything happened to you, your children wouldn't give me anything. They'd throw me out in the street."

That really bothered me. I said, "How can you be asking me to make a contract? I'm the one who should have done it before we got married. Do you remember how you were when you first came to my house? You didn't even have a job!"

He said, "Yes, but I'm going to help you with the work in the restaurant and in the apartments. And if you don't help me by signing some papers, I'm going to feel up in the air. I won't be able to throw myself into the work."

I thought, *He's probably right. Maybe that's the way to avoid any problems.*

And since he was working so hard, I never said anything to my family. And like a big fool, there I went to the lawyer, and we made the contract. Later I asked him, "Are you happy now?"

He said, "Of course! Thank you. Now I'll work more willingly."

Well, it seems that day I signed my own death sentence. The business continued to prosper. In a few more months, my husband didn't want to work in the kitchen anymore. He wanted to be a waiter, and that's where the problems began. How could he be a waiter if he didn't speak English? And the customers began to complain to my children, and my children began to complain to me. They said he had to learn to speak English before he could be a waiter. Well, some days he worked as a waiter and others as a busboy, but he didn't want to work in the kitchen anymore.

At about that time, we had only eight months left on our restaurant contract, and the owner of the building said that he wouldn't keep renting to us and that if we wanted the business, he would rent us the building but that we had to buy all the equipment. And he wanted to double the rent and sell the equipment for twice what it was worth. Well, I decided we would have to leave when the contract was over.

During that time, a man came into the restaurant to ask me if we wanted to sign a lease for a new place in a shopping center they were going to put up in a better business area than where we were but only two miles away from there. I talked with my children and with my husband, and we all agreed that it would be better, so we signed the lease. I got together all the information that he requested, and we signed everything. They told us that when our current lease was up, the shopping center would be ready and we could move in. So then we started to try to get a loan. I had to do it alone because my husband didn't have the experience, the insurance, or the immigration papers. My daughter Gloria and I were busy with all the preparations for the loan, equipment, and plans for how I wanted the kitchen to be. There were only two months left before we had to turn the business over, and the new shopping center barely had the foundations laid. We were very worried because we were all going to be without work. What were we going to do?

While we were worrying about that, my cousin Manuel Valencia came to eat at the restaurant, and I told him what was happening to us. He said, "Don't worry, cousin. I know a little restaurant where somebody opened a taco shop that went broke, and now it's closed."

It was in Livingston, and he said that I could enlarge the place. And I said to him, "But, Manuel, back to Livingston? I can't believe it! Why is life so difficult for me?"

But what were we going to do? My son Rafael was studying medicine in St. Louis, Missouri, and it was costing me a lot of money each month. I had to pay his rent and buy him clothes. Although he was working a little and they had given him a scholarship, it wasn't enough.

Returning to the Past

So we had to go back to Livingston. Two months before we turned over the place in Ceres, my husband began to fix up the place in Livingston so that we could move. Some other people and I also worked very hard to get the place ready and make it look pretty. It was really small, but thank God, my customers followed me wherever I went. That's how I went back to the town where four years earlier my business had gone up in smoke. I stayed there eight months. During those eight months, I worked every day with two of my other employees. All of my Livingston friends and previous customers were very happy that I had returned. A lot of clients from Modesto came to visit me and to eat in Livingston. They kept saying to me, "Lupe, when are you going to open in Ceres? We're waiting for you!"

Other people told me that if I opened a restaurant under a tree, I'd have customers there because they liked my food!

When the other place in the shopping center in Ceres was ready, I got an unpleasant surprise. When we were about to open, an inspector went to check the place out. We already had everything installed and were planning to open in three days, but the inspector put a note on the main door saying that we couldn't open until we had installed an emergency door. That delayed our opening, and I lost three months because the original plans were not done correctly.

Laughter and Tears

I cried buckets of tears because I couldn't open on time. But when we finally did open, my customers were waiting for me with open arms. After all those problems, we opened and the restaurant filled up immediately. At that moment, Javier and my husband came from the bank saying that I had to go pick up the loan check and that it was only part of the whole amount they had said they would loan me. And that day, I was supposed to pay for the restaurant equipment and some work that had been done, and the people were waiting for their money. When my son told me what had happened, I couldn't stand so many things at once. I couldn't cook because I was crying so much I was almost drowning. I couldn't believe it. Full of anguish, I left the other helper in the kitchen and went to talk with my accountant, Carlos Vergara. He is an excellent person. I said to him, "Tell me what to do. I can't stand it anymore."

He answered, "Lupe, please calm down. I'll talk to the people that you were going to pay today. They'll just have to wait. What else can they do? Give me the phone numbers of the people you were going to pay today."

And that's what happened. It was a big relief for me. I'll never forget him and I am always going to be grateful to him. I went back and cooked more peacefully after talking to him. That's one reason my friendships have such a big place in my heart.

That was the beginning of a huge success. One could say that it was incredible, but with the help of God, everything is possible.

Then my husband took charge of the business in Livingston, and I was in Ceres with fourteen employees. I had debts, lots of debts, but I also had a great desire to provide an education for my children and to make all my dreams come true. One the other hand, my husband was making a mess of the accounting in Livingston now that he thought he was the boss and the owner. Two of his sisters and four other young and pretty girls worked there. Just imagine, in less than a year, he didn't have enough money to pay the business bills! He almost never worked. The cooks called me in Ceres constantly, saying that they needed things and he wasn't around.

Well, the problems became more frequent. The cooks called me to say that the workers were fighting among themselves. And to top it off, one day, my husband came to the Ceres business where I was working. We had two telephones, one outside in the dining room and another in the kitchen. I realized that he had been talking for a long time, and I picked up the kitchen telephone and heard him flirting with one of the waitresses that worked in Livingston. I told them both that they didn't have a drop of decency and a lot of other things. That day, I had a really ugly fight with him. At that very moment, I told the girl she was fired and to get out. But the problems continued. He paid no attention to the business. On the other hand, things were going well in Ceres. I worked every day and double shifts on the weekends, as always. My daughter Gloria and my son Javier also helped me a lot with the business. And in less than a year, I paid all the bills that I had, and we had enough money left over to go on vacation for a week in Hawaii at Christmastime.

Christmas in Hawaii

I was really exhausted from so much work. I had only taken one day off in the whole year. We went with another couple who were good friends. My children stayed home to take care of the business. Well, there in Hawaii, my husband didn't behave very well. We went to one of those parties they have there, with food and drinks all included in the same price. My husband drank so much that we had to drag him out of the place. He spent the whole night in the bathroom. I actually thought he was going to die. The next day, we were supposed to go on a tour and we had already paid for the trip. But how could he go? He had spent the night sick in the bathroom. I went to a store and bought him some food and juice, and I said to him, "I hope God will look after you. I'm going with my friend and her husband."

And he answered, "That's okay."

But really I didn't even enjoy myself, hoping that nothing bad was happening to him. When he got back, he was feeling better. In spite of everything, we had a good time. We visited some beautiful places.

When we got back from vacation, my relatives Ana and Lupe Montanez wanted to buy the Livingston restaurant from me. They already had a restaurant in Turlock, and I had let them use my name there, so they wanted to buy the one in Livingston as well. We thought it was a good idea to sell it, especially since we had so many problems there.

Well, on one hand, things got better, and on the other, they got worse. My husband didn't want to work in the kitchen, and the waiters didn't want to work with him. I got complaints from all directions. Then in order to avoid more quarrels, my husband just worked as a cashier on the weekends, and he took charge of the rents at the apartments. But then my son Javier, who was the only one still at home besides the baby, began to complain that he couldn't stand my husband because everything seemed wrong to that man. My husband even said that my son was stealing money from the business, and my children, in spite of everything, had treated him respectfully, but nothing seemed to satisfy him.

Well, I was already too tired. My husband bothered my son so much that he left the house and went to live with a friend of his. I was really angry and upset about that. We had so many arguments that I really couldn't take it anymore. One day, I decided to speak seriously to my husband. I told him that I really couldn't stand it anymore, that I was going to get a divorce, and that he should live his own life and I would live mine. But when I told him this in all seriousness, he began to cry like a baby, begging my pardon. He said he loved me and his daughter very much and asked how I could want to separate from him. When I saw him crying and being repentant, I truly thought he was sincere, and we hugged each other and cried together.

That day, I decided that life was full of problems and wondered why I should live my whole life suffering. If it wasn't one thing, it would be another, and I ought to trust him. And anyway, even if my son had left my house, he was still working in the restaurant. And I told myself, "No more suffering. I'm going to be happy."

My business had become well known, and I didn't have to work so much. So if my husband wanted to work, okay, and if not, it was also okay. By now, we had very good employees, and my children also took care of the business. That was in 1987, when the Amnesty law passed and my husband and all of his brothers and sisters were able to apply for amnesty. I wrote letters confirming their work for all of them and also for my employees who weren't legal. So now everything seemed to be pure happiness. We frequently went on trips to different parts of California and we often went to Reno, Nevada, to gamble in the casinos. That year in June, we went to a casino, and I won $17,200 on a quarter machine. It was a big surprise, especially since I had never earned any money that easily before. And my husband said to me immediately, "Don't share the money with your children. Let them work! They're young."

And that's what happened. I only gave one hundred dollars to each of them.

Vacation in the Hospital

Near the end of 1987, my husband received his permanent residency card. Immediately, he said to me, "Let's go to my town in Mexico to visit my relatives. It's been seven years since I was there."

First, we were going to Cancun, Mexico, for a week. My husband, Erica, and I left on the first of December. The day after we arrived in beautiful Cancun, we went on an excursion to see the beaches and Mayan pyramids. We were very happy. Three days later, Erica got a terrible pain in her stomach, along with a high fever, diarrhea, and vomiting. I became very frightened, and we called a doctor. She was seriously ill, and the doctor said, "You have to take her to the clinic and get her an intravenous supplement. Her fever is very high."

Well, we took her immediately, and they attended to her instantly. My husband went out to bring me something to eat and drink. After about three hours, he came back and said, "I'm going to the hotel. Why should we both stay here?"

I stayed with the child all night long, begging God to make her well. The next day, at about noon, the doctor came in and said, "The child is much better. The fever has broken. You can go now. I'm going to give you some more medicine for her to take."

Well then, I called my husband at the hotel, but he wasn't there. He hadn't called me or gone to the clinic since the previous night. I couldn't believe it. I called the hotel to tell them that I was going there so that they would open the door for me. Then the doctor from the clinic said, "I'll take you to the hotel."

When we arrived, my husband wasn't there. When he arrived, he told me he had gone to look for us, and I said to him, "I don't understand you. You didn't even call to find out about your daughter."

"Why? You and the doctors were there with her."

And I answered, "How could you be so calm?"

I couldn't believe it. Well, the next day, we left by plane for his town, Churintzio, Michoacán. It was the first time that I had gone there. All of his sisters that were there, his parents, and his relatives treated me like a queen. They almost wanted to put food in my mouth personally. The three weeks that we were there, we went to see many nearby places. In Churintzio, facing the house of my in-laws was a house for sale. It was far from being finished, and the owner was selling it a for very reasonable price. It was a two-story house, and I really liked it. From the front of the house, there was a view of some pools and a mountain. All of the windows already had decorative iron bars. I said to my husband, "Why don't we buy that house with the money I won in the casino in Reno? We'll fix it up so that it will be very pretty."

He said, "I like the idea. That way, when we take vacation a couple times a year, we'll have a place to come to."

Well, we went to talk to the owner and we made a deal. Then we went back to California to get the money to buy the house. Three weeks later, we went to Mexico again to pay for the house and sign the papers. I wanted to have certain changes made to the interior, and we went to buy the materials to finish the house. I wanted everything to be as pretty as possible. I wanted the bedrooms and the living room carpeted and the baths tiled and the corridors and the kitchen with marble floors. I chose all the colors I liked and all the sinks and toilets. After we bought everything, my husband said, "Look, Lupe, if you want, I'll stay here in Mexico with my parents to tell the workers what to do, everything that you want them to change in the house. And I'll help them too. We can finish the house in about two months, and you can go look after the business and the apartments."

Well, I returned to California with no worries because he was going to stay with his parents. He stayed there for two and a half months. I sent him money whenever he needed something for the house. He returned to California on April 15, 1988. My daughter and I were really happy that he was coming. We even went and bought him a dozen balloons, and I bought him a gold bracelet. I had really made the garden of the house look pretty. I wanted everything to be as nice as possible for his return. I guess it's because I was in love, especially since his entire family had treated me so well in his town. I felt very happy because my husband called me from San Francisco to say that he was on his way.

He arrived that night with his mother. He seemed very happy to me. He told me all about the house and everything that he had done. That night, when we went to bed, we didn't enjoy the intimacy that I expected. He was very cold to me. He said he was very tired from the flight. He turned his back on me and fell asleep, or at least that's what it seemed like. That night, I didn't say anything but I could hardly sleep, thinking that something must have happened in Mexico.

The next day, I didn't go to the restaurant. I made him breakfast, and then he left. He was going to deliver something that had been sent from his town. He said that he wouldn't be long. I said to myself, "I'm going to cook him something special for dinner."

So I prepared a stew and a cake too. And how do you think he surprised me? He didn't come back until very late that night and didn't even phone me! And I didn't even eat. I got really mad as I waited for him, even though I didn't want to fight with him. He came in as if nothing had happened. I said to him, "What happened to you? I cooked you something special and I made a cake, too, but you never came. At least, you could have called me."

"Excuse me," he said. "It just got late."

But I felt that something was really wrong. Two weeks later, we went with some friends to Las Vegas, Nevada, for three days, and I forgot about the change in him. And that same year, we went on a cruise with my daughter Gloria, her husband and children, and another couple who were our friends. The cruise lasted a week and went from Acapulco to Los Angeles, California. But during all those months from April to December, he seemed to be in another world. He got mad for any foolish reason. Sometimes it even made me laugh. He would be gone all day, and when I would ask where he had been, he would answer that he didn't have to give me any explanations about where he went. And he was almost always bothered by something. Well, we went on the cruise, and he was acting very strangely toward me. He didn't even want to go dancing, and I would say to him, "Well, what's the matter with you? We came to enjoy ourselves!"

After we came back from the cruise, one of our cooks went on vacation, and I had to work every day until she got back. One day, one of my employees said, "You know, Lupe, you work too much, and your husband is never here. He doesn't even come to the restaurant. Don't you think you give him too much freedom? If I were you, I'd keep closer tabs on him."

It turns out that they knew he was seeing a young woman and that sometimes they even went to the restaurant to eat, but they didn't want to tell me because they didn't want me to suffer. And I answered, "If he's doing anything wrong, sooner or later I'll find out."

Well, when the cook got back from her vacation, a sister and a brother of my husband's invited us to Reno, Nevada, to play in the casinos. My husband didn't want to go. He said, "Go if you want. I don't want to go."

That was on January 17, 1989. I went with my sister and brother-in-law. Well, I'm never going to forget that day. The trip lasted three hours, and the only topic of conversation was my brother's wife. They said she was a worthless person who didn't respect anybody. Because of the things they were telling me, that made me understand that she hadn't respected my relationship with my husband either. They said that they had seen her kissing someone but that they would never tell me who it was. My sister-in-law also told me not to let my brother's wife come to my house because she was so shameless. Needless to say, I didn't enjoy myself at all in the casinos. I even had a few drinks. The day seemed an eternity to me. When we got home, I asked my husband if he had been the one who was kissing my brother's wife, and he just laughed and said it wasn't true. But I didn't believe him and I began to investigate. I went to see a cousin of mine who lives in Livingston because at that time, she was working in the restaurant in Livingston that I had sold. And she also worked with my brother's wife.

CHAPTER 5

From Bad to Worse

Cruel Deception

MY COUSIN TOLD ME THAT it was true that they found my sister-in-law kissing my husband but that I shouldn't worry because it had happened almost two years ago. I was so mad I just felt like I was going to die. He denied everything, but I knew it was true. That same day, I spoke to my brother's wife. They were separated, and I had let her live in one of my apartments, almost free, because I pitied her. Besides that, they had lived in my own house for a few months when they first came from Mexico, and I had given them both work in my restaurants. How could she be so cruel and unfeeling? That very day, I told her to get out of the apartment and said that I never wanted to see her in my house again.

And because I was really hurt, I kept on investigating. I waited desperately for the phone bill to see if my husband had been calling her, because it was a long-distance call. Well, I found a different phone number. There were several calls, and I realized that they were made when I was working, so I called to find out who was making those calls from my house. The person who answered said that nobody was, but I noticed my husband was looking very nervous.

My cousin Maria lived in Livingston, so I went there to ask her about the phone number. She was the one who told me everything. She said the number belonged to a young woman who was separated from her husband, and the woman had also been in Mexico when my husband was there, right in the same town where my husband had stayed to fix up the house. My cousin gave me all the information I needed—the young woman's name, where she lived, everything. So apparently for about a year, my husband had been seeing this woman behind my back, and I knew nothing about it. All of my employees already knew about it. Well, the day that I discovered my husband was truly unfaithful to me, the first thing I thought of was committing suicide. I didn't want any more to do with this rotten world.

I went home with my heart broken into a thousand pieces, thinking that my life was ruined. My illusions were destroyed. I had fought with myself to believe in that man, and it was all for nothing. I was willing to put up with a lot from him, but I could never share him with another woman. I had a lot of womanly pride. All I could think of that day when I went home with a bottle of strong liquor was hugging my baby daughter, kissing her with all my might, and driving my car right into a tree.

When I got home, my husband was sitting in front of the TV. There was a vase on the dining room table. I threw it at him but I didn't hit him. And I said to him, "What did you think I was? The most stupid woman in the world?"

That was really the end! I went to my daughter Erica's room, kissed and hugged her, and went running out to the car. But my husband figured out what I wanted to do, and he stopped me. He took the car keys away from me, and since he was stronger than I was, I couldn't resist. And then he told me what he called the whole truth. He said that he had been going with that woman but that they had broken up. I was a complete wreck. How could I believe such a lie after seeing the phone bill and all the calls he made from my own house? I was shouting like a wild woman. My daughter Esmeralda called, and I just grabbed the phone and threw it to the floor without even finding out who it was. I cried and cried. I felt more rage and pain than I had ever felt. I thought such double dealing was impossible!

Then in about two minutes, my two daughters, Esmeralda and Gloria, and Jorge, Esmeralda's husband, got to my house. They took my husband outside, and my daughters tried to console me, but it was no help. I wanted to die. I didn't want to keep on living! That's because I always wanted to believe that he sincerely loved me and that we were happy. For me, it was just like death. I know that I couldn't keep living with him anymore. All the love and respect I had felt for him was destroyed in that moment. My daughters told me that these things happened every day to married couples, that I shouldn't try to end it all, and that I should think of all my children and the baby. That we should to see a priest who would give us advice. But what could a priest do? It wouldn't change what my heart felt.

The next to arrive was Rafael, my son who was studying to be a doctor. He was only two years away from graduating. He said to me, "Mom, I'm sure that you're not going to be able to go on living with that man. The best thing would be for you to see a counselor."

He asked me to promise him that I would go. But the worst thing was that I couldn't sleep. I had a headache that didn't go away for a second no matter what I took. I went to the doctor about ten days later, and he had to give me a shot that made me sleep for twenty-four hours. But as soon as the medication wore off, I felt the same way again.

Divorce Papers

Then I went to see a counselor, and when he saw me drowning in tears, he said, "What you have to do is go see a lawyer and get a divorce. You can't go on with that man. If you don't do something, you'll fall apart completely. Ask for a divorce and tell him to get out of the house. Be alone for a while, and then time will tell."

So that's what I did. I went to see a lawyer and I started the process, and it seemed like what was happening to me didn't even matter to my husband. My daughters said, "Why don't you just send him to Mexico for a few months so that you can think about whether you want to forgive him or not?"

Then my husband went to see the lawyer and picked up the divorce papers. I asked him to go to Mexico, and he went, but he took my son-in-law Jorge to help him build some staircases in the house we had bought. Well, every time he phoned me, we did nothing but fight. His mother wrote to me and told me that I had to get back together with him, that all men cheated on their wives. That made me even madder. They didn't care what I was going through, because if I left her son, they wouldn't keep on getting the money I sent and wouldn't be able to take advantage of us. I didn't answer her letter. I felt totally wounded.

When my husband came back, he didn't get balloons or presents. We talked for a long time, because before I found out that he was cheating on me, we had made a lot of plans. We had bought the house in Mexico and we had also bought another house here in Turlock and a lot to build a very big house in one of the best parts of Turlock. We already had the plans drawn up. He asked me to give him another chance. Well, we stayed together for a little while longer, but we were both always fighting about everything. There was simply no more trust.

At that time, my son Javier was buying a house, and I was going to help him with some of the money for the down payment. My husband had known that all along. Well, when I mentioned the money I was going to give Javier, my husband got madder than I had ever seen him. He shouted at me, and I shouted back. He said we'd be better off apart. So then I went to the lawyer to sign all the papers. At that time, I was going to give him one of the houses, half of the money we had saved, his truck, his tools, and a motorcycle. I was also going to give him one hundred thousand dollars in payments because I was going to keep all the apartments, the house in Mexico, the lot where we were going to build, and the restaurant. When my husband saw that I was really going to do it, he started crying, and so did I.

He left at night when our baby daughter was sleeping. She didn't know we were separated. That started another problem. The child really loved her father a lot, and I still loved him. Besides, there was the problem of his family and one of his sisters who worked in my restaurant. She told me every day how much her brother was crying over me and his daughter, saying that he was truly repentant. And then he would call me up, crying, and I cried just as much. I don't think there is any power stronger than love. Well, love won out, and within a week, I let him come back. Another big mistake in my life!

I went and stopped the divorce proceedings. That was in May of 1989. I did all I could to try to forget what had happened. That same year, we went to Churintzio, in Mexico, to finish the house. His family kept on treating me as if nothing had happened. We were there six weeks. They finished the house, and we furnished it with the best of everything. We took a lot of things from California. We furnished it with the prettiest things we could find—paintings and plants and flowers—because we weren't worried about anything. His parents and sisters who lived across the street were going to take care of the house. Besides, it was very safe there. The people in that town are very happy. They have a lot of parties in the month of December. They have posadas and bring in bands and set off fireworks. I was very taken with the house. After they finished it, I spent a lot of time cleaning and decorating it. I thought of every little detail. My daughter Erica loved to go to Churintzio because there were so many good people there. But you know what? We only slept in the new house for three nights before we returned to California, but we were happy that we had completely finished the house and that it would be there when we went back again.

We returned home in September. In about a month, the State of California bought the apartment property that I had in Livingston alongside Highway 99 because they were going to build a bridge. They paid me well, and with that money, I began to build my dream house. But my husband and I continued to have problems. He began to drink heavily. He was drinking in the house and everywhere else we went. That year, we were godparents at several weddings. Sometimes we got mad at each other and didn't enjoy ourselves at all, and he began to ignore me. We would go out for a walk, and he would walk as far away from me as he could. And he began to shout at me, at times even in front of other people. When we were building the house, we had a lot of quarrels. He wanted one thing, and I wanted another. Some days we didn't even speak to each other. Our daughter was also very nervous. The situation got worse each day.

My Dream House

We finished my dream house at the end of August 1990, and we moved in. It took a lot of work to organize everything. The house we had before my dream house was also very pretty. It had a swimming pool and a Jacuzzi, but it was only one story. It had three bedrooms, two baths, a living room, and a kitchen. But my dream house was really big. It has five bedrooms, four baths, two living rooms, two dining rooms, and a four-car garage. It also had a swimming pool and a Jacuzzi. I designed it to suit my taste, inside and out.

Well, we barely moved into the new house, and one Sunday, when I left work, I told my husband to give me the money to take care of the bills, as I always did. I always let him know about all the payments and all the sales. That day, he said he wouldn't give me the money and said that from then on, I wasn't going to manage our finances. He said he would give me money for my expenses but only once a week. He was going to do the accounting and go to the bank and that if I went to the bank, he would count the money first. Then I asked him, "What's the matter with you? Have you gone crazy? What makes you think that I'm going to work like a slave and never touch the money?

He answered, "If you don't want it to be like that, give me my half and I'll go to the other house."

He also told me that I was no longer really needed at the restaurant. He said that the cooks now knew how to cook very well and that the customers didn't come to see my "pretty face." The people came because they liked the food. Well, that was worse than getting a knife stuck in my heart. How could my husband throw me out of my own business? He didn't even know how to cook! That whole day was one really big fight. I cried disconsolately. The only thing I really considered my own was the business that had cost me so much sacrifice and so many headaches, and now that my food was famous, my own husband was throwing me out. That took the cake! But I hurt so much that I said to him, "Keep the business. Let's see how long you can last. And when you need a cook, you'll have to cook."

But it seemed like the devil had gotten into him. At that time, my daughter Gloria was the manager because she spoke fluent English. Besides, she has studied at the university. I also wanted her to profit from the business because she had helped me so much.

My other daughter, Esmeralda, also had a restaurant. Well, I didn't want to tell my children anything about what happened between my husband and me. I just stopped going to the restaurant. When they asked me about it, I told them that I was fixing up the house. But my daughter didn't believe me, and one day, she came to the house and said, "I want to know what's going on, Mom. I know that something is wrong, but if you don't go to the restaurant tomorrow, all the workers are leaving, and I'll go with them. What happened to all your strength? Are you going to let yourself be completely destroyed?"

I just cried. She said, "I won't work one day longer if you don't go back. Neither will all the employees. Everybody's leaving. You decide. Are you going to let somebody destroy everything that you worked so hard for, beginning from we didn't even have enough money to buy food? You're letting that man destroy you and do whatever he wants with you." Gloria continued, "You've always been strong. Why are you giving in to a person who doesn't love you and is just tearing you apart?"

Well, the next day, I got ready and I went to the restaurant. I went in and said to my husband, "Your shift is over. I'm here to work. This is my shift." Then I added, "And it's my business."

And he said, "Fine," and he left.

And I stayed, working as the cashier. When I got home that night, he was really angry. He said he wanted to go to the house that we had recently left because I was giving money to my children behind his back. And he wanted his share, what was coming to him. I showed him the door and told him it was there whenever he wanted to leave, but he answered, "Before I go, I want my share. I'm not leaving here until you give me my share."

I was just a bundle of nerves. I saw very clearly that he didn't want to live with me. And what would happen to the house in Mexico and everything else? Besides, what were Erica and I going to do alone in that huge two-story house? Suddenly, my whole world seemed to turn black. I finally said to him that instead of always fighting over everything, we should go to Churintzio, Michoacán, even if it was just for a month, at least to enjoy the house. We had bought a new pickup with a double cab. That seemed like a good idea to him, and so we decided to take a vacation. And we went in the pickup, even though we usually traveled by plane. That way, we could see a lot of places. His sister who worked with me also thought it was a good idea. At the end of November 1990, my husband and I, our child, and my husband's sister set out. I was thinking, *I hope to God that this trip helps us and makes him think straight because a divorce is hell.*

Well, everything went well while we were on the road. It was a lot of fun. We stopped and slept in hotels because we only drove during the day. We got to his town in December. They have very nice festivities there that traditionally last from December 7 to December 12. The band plays in the streets every day. They celebrate the Day of the Virgin of Guadalupe. They have posadas, in which people reenact the story of Mary and Joseph, going from home to home seeking shelter until they are finally admitted to one of the houses. They build floats and decorate the streets with cords and plants. I also held a posada at my house.

Besides that, I took part in another posada. I got dressed as a *guare* with skirts with a lot of ruffles and lots of necklaces. And it was really funny to see me with a stone metate and a comal with fake flames. We had dough in the metate, as if we were making tortillas. Five other little girls dressed as *guares* near me pretended to be eating tortillas, and others were making chili in a stone molcajete. And we had real chilies and tomatoes in the comal. A lot of people filmed us, and a lot of them that go to the fiestas in Mexico also knew me and they would say, "Morenita, we want to eat. Give us some nice hot tortillas because just seeing you make tortillas and grind chili makes us hungry."

It was a lot of fun.

Family Reunion

One thing I can say, for sure, is that a lot of people are going to remember me in Churintzio, Michoacán, because many of them are really fine people. I made a lot of friends, and my family in Aguililla called me to say that they were coming to visit me in Churintzio to see the house that we had bought. Besides, I had never said anything to my father about the problems with my husband. I didn't want him to worry—not because he's my father but because he's a good person. The last thing I wanted was to make my family suffer.

After the festivities, my father, my brothers and sisters, and my stepmother came from Aguililla to visit us in Churintzio. Those who came were my stepmother, Adelina Franco, and my brothers and sisters—Juan Cordoba, Adela Cordoba, Rosa Cordoba, and Angelica Cordoba. They're the children from my father's second marriage. When they were in my house, my father and they were really happy. They liked the house that we bought very much. We decided to go with them to the seacoast at Playa Azul, which is near Zihuatanejo and Acapulco. My father, my brothers and sisters, my mother-in-law, and one of her sisters had never been there. We really had a good time with the whole family. I tried to enjoy myself, but inside a voice kept saying, "This may be the last time you go on vacation with your husband," because his mind seemed to be someplace else far away.

He was serious, almost angry. I couldn't say anything to him because everything I said bothered him. That's how things went. He ignored me. Sometimes he didn't even notice me. I felt totally disillusioned. The person I had met when he was suffering dire poverty was now humiliating me so much! But I was seeing everything more clearly. He didn't love me, and I had to give him his freedom. Why would I want to keep somebody against his will? It's like doing oneself in.

We went back to Churintzio. My father and his family left for Aguililla, and I thought about my house, so pretty and welcoming, just like all the pretty things I had bought for the house. My husband's parents and sisters were always showing off the house to all their friends, acting as if it were theirs. I thought, if my husband doesn't want to live with me and he leaves, I'll never see this house again.

That hurt me a lot. I cried in silence and begged God to give me strength, to help me, to not leave me alone. I could see another deep abyss opening up in my life. My daughter Erica was only ten years old and very close to me. She needed me a lot, more than my other children. Well, we went back to California after New Year's Day. My husband's sister stayed there in Churintzio. We were angry all along the road and barely spoke to each other. When we got to Turlock, I went to the restaurant, and my daughter Gloria said, "Mom, you don't look very happy. It looks like you went to a funeral instead of going on vacation."

I answered, "Something like that."

She asked, "Are the problems still there?"

And I answered, "There's no way to cure them."

Soon after we arrived, we had another big discussion. He told me clearly that he only wanted his share before leaving the house to go to the other house that I had bought before marrying him. And he also said that I shouldn't ask anything of him because he wasn't going to accommodate me. That we had been together for ten years but there was no more love. That I should decide. He only wanted his share before leaving the house.

Then I reached my limit. I asked him how much he wanted in order to get this nightmare over with once and for all. I couldn't sleep and I didn't feel right anywhere. Well, when he told me everything that he wanted me to give him, I almost had a heart attack. I couldn't believe it. That man really wanted to destroy me inside and out. He wanted to leave me in total ruins. I felt so much rage and pain that I could hardly stand it. I began to sob. I said to him, "You've gone crazy."

But I didn't know that man. He was like a monster. I said, "You're probably capable of killing me just to keep everything. But don't forget, there's a contract."

And he answered, "It doesn't matter to me."

At that time, we had three houses plus my dream house and the restaurant business. He said to me, "I want the three houses or your dream house. You choose. And I want three thousand dollars a month from the businesses for as long as you have the restaurant, plus you finish paying off the pickup, and, of course, half of our savings and half of the money owed to us."

What do you think of that? I shouted like a wild woman and said, "You're crazy. I don't believe it! How can you do this to me? Is this the way you've decided to show your love for my daughter and me?" I had believed his tears the first time we separated for a week, and I had gone back with him. But now he answered without any sympathy, "Well, you were hardly going to give me any money. That's why I was crying."

This time, not a tear fell because he was determined to get what he wanted. There was no crying for him. I told him that even if he died, I wouldn't give him my dream house or the three thousand dollars a month from the business because my daughter and I had to eat. And besides, he said very clearly that he wasn't going to give our daughter any money because I was going to keep the restaurant. Right then, my daughter Erica shouted at us, saying that she couldn't sleep. She had heard everything from a window in the second story of the house. I thought she was asleep.

We stopped there. We hadn't made a deal. I went to bed with my daughter, who was only ten years old and was very nervous and frightened. I didn't sleep a wink. Very early the next day, before taking Erica to school, my husband told me, "I want you to go to the lawyer today and set everything up."

And I answered, "I'm not going to give you three thousand dollars a month. Do you think I'm going to work just for you? What are we going to live on? And why should I give you the three houses? Why don't you give the house in Mexico to your daughter Erica?"

And he answered, "She doesn't need that house for anything."

Well, we both cried as if someone had died. Then my husband said, "Look, then give me the three houses and everything else I told you, and $80,000 from the business in payments, but we've got to settle everything today."

He already had an appointment with an attorney because mine wasn't going to be in that day. I went to the restaurant, and I called my lawyer from there. As it happens, I was able to find him and explain the situation, even though he already knew about it. I hoped that he would help me and see how abusive my husband was being and how unfair it was. Well, I made an appointment and I took all the papers for the houses, but I didn't say anything to my daughters Gloria and Esmeralda. I didn't want any more problems, and my sons weren't close by. Rafael was in another state, in New York, doing medical research, and my son Javier had gone to a seminary in Switzerland for six months. So I went to the lawyer alone.

A Huge Disillusionment

Well, in spite of my tears and all, the lawyer didn't help me at all! It seems like he sold out. He told me that I was coming out ahead because I was going to keep the business, and the new house was worth much more than the other two houses, and the house in Mexico didn't count here in California. I thought then that only God could help me. I told the lawyer that I had the business long before I married my husband and that we had built my dream house with some money that we had not earned together. That money was from the sale of the property that I had bought before knowing him. Well, it did me no good. He said I didn't have any prenuptial agreement showing separate property and that he couldn't help me out at all. Instead of looking for another attorney or asking for more information so I could understand, I was so full of rage and pain at that moment that I signed over the papers for the three houses he wanted, and we agreed on his terms for the contract—the money I was going to give him and the rest of the things he was taking, like the motorcycle and his tools.

I signed over everything I was going to give him and wanted him to leave my house forever. I don't know where I got the strength to go on living. When I told my daughters, they almost had a heart attack. They even cried. How could I have given him so much! And I was still going to pay him $80,000 from the business in payments! They said to me, "You're crazy too, Mom. You've just given that worthless person what you earned from all your years of work and sacrifice and ours too."

And I answered, "Everything's all signed. I can't do anything about it now."

That was on January 26, 1991. I was truly broken up. I shut myself up in my house. For several days, I didn't want to see anybody. I didn't want to do any more explaining. If anybody came to comfort me, I wouldn't open the door. The only people I would see were my friend Lupita, my daughters, and a niece, Ana Montanez. Three days after the separation, my niece Ana called me and said, "Auntie, how can you be giving so much to that man? Please, Auntie, even if you already signed over the houses to him and you gave him half the money, don't give him any more. How can you possibly give him $80,000 more? Auntie, you did it in a moment of anguish and desperation. Don't give him anything else, please! Talk to your lawyer and tell him that you aren't going to give out any more money. The lawyer didn't help you. He just told you that you were coming out ahead. That's not true. He lied to you. You've worked so many years so hard just so that terrible man can take almost everything away from you."

My niece knew what I had suffered to achieve what I had. She had worked with me in the restaurant for a long time. Well, I paid attention to my niece and to my daughters who were crying because of their sadness and despair. And that very minute, I called my lawyer. I was really angry. I said that instead of helping me, he had sent me up the creek and that I wasn't going to give any more money to my husband, even if he killed me. I told him not to even think that thought! If he had already sent the papers to court, I said, "You may know what you're doing, but I'm not going to pay my husband even one more cent!"

And he answered, "Well, your husband can take you to court."

And I said, "Well, let him. But no more money."

Then the lawyer said, "Don't count on me for anything."

I answered, "I don't need you."

But my husband, a week after we separated, was already at a wedding with the same woman he's sworn that he'd broken up with two years ago. I heard the gossip immediately. Well then, a flame shot through my body, and I grabbed the phone and called my husband and told him I wouldn't give him another cent. If he wanted money, he should go to work, and I wasn't going to pay for his pickup. Not even if I were crazy. And he answered, "We'll see about that!"

He said it would be better if I deposited the money in the bank every month as I had agreed because if I didn't do it, he was going to take me to court. I was so angry that I told him to do whatever he wanted, but I wasn't going to give him any more money, even if I died! But I really thought he would dare take me to court. I couldn't believe that he was so cruel. Well, you're not going to believe it, but when he didn't get any money for two months, he called me up and said, "You better put the money in the bank for me if you don't want to go to court."

And I answered, "Don't you understand Spanish? Do you want me to say it in another language? I'm not giving you any more money. You'll have to put me out to live on the street first."

Well, who could believe that man would sell even his soul to the devil for money? One week later, I got a summons to go to court. Immediately I had to hire a good lawyer that a friend recommended.

That's when I really cried black tears. I couldn't believe it. For me, it was impossible to accept such evil-mindedness. How could I believe that the man that I allowed to live in my house when I brought him from Tijuana, all sick and without a cent, was going to take me to court for money after all he had already taken? At the same time, I was prepared to fight to define what was mine to the last minute. He had already taken too much away from me, and I wasn't going to allow him to continue to destroy me.

Well, the lawyer that I hired asked me for so much information and so much money to take the case that my daughter Gloria had to help me fill out all the papers. And when we went to take all the information to the lawyer, I found out something terrible that my daughter Gloria had written—that shameless man has stepped out of bounds with her one time when he dropped Erica off so Gloria could babysit her. Gloria was already married, and he didn't do anything because she put him in his place. And my daughter Gloria never told me anything in order to avoid problems with her husband, Marcos. That really hurt me a lot in the depths of my soul.

How could they have let me live with a man who didn't even respect my own family? Although it happened seven years before I found out about it, it still hurt a lot. It was the worst of the worst. It was something I could never forgive. I found out about so many things that he did behind my back that I had never imagined. It seems like when we're in love, we're truly blind. I was blind. I didn't see beyond the tip of my nose.

Well, after we gave testimony for the court, they delayed the court hearing. I really felt that I couldn't stand so much disillusionment, and I asked my daughter Esmeralda and my son-in-law Jorge if they could go with Erica, the grandchildren, and me to the beach at Mazatlán, Mexico, for a few days. And that's what we did. We went in April 1991. I was like a crazy person. I walked along the seashore every morning. I swam in the ocean. I sunbathed, but inside I was fighting very hard just to not die from the pain I was feeling. I thought about all the love I had felt for my husband's family and the love that they had shown me, which was a phony love because they never even called me on the phone, not even to say they were sorry about what was happening. Nothing. Everything had ended. My husband's mother only came to see her granddaughter two times in four years. My thoughts seemed like a record that kept playing the same tune over and over.

I cried about my house in Mexico for a year because I had built it with love, so much love, so we could go there and rest on our vacations. And how much had I enjoyed that house and all my things? Just five weeks! That wasn't fair because he kept the house and everything in it. So the record in my brain got badly scratched. We spent ten days in Mazatlán and we returned to Turlock.

The day of the court hearing arrived, and they delayed it for about six months. Even before we went to court, my daughter Erica didn't want to see her father anymore. Every time she went, she came home crying and saying to me that she didn't want to see her father. And I kept thinking, *I have to do something that will help me out of this nightmare.*

One day, my son-in-law Jorge and my daughter Esmeralda invited me on an excursion to the mountains near Sonora, California. And there high up in the mountains, right off Highway 108, there was a restaurant for sale, and we went to see how much they wanted for it. We checked with the real estate agency, and they told us the price. Then they showed it to us, and I thought it was very pretty, surrounded by green pine trees. And my son-in-law said to me, "Buy it and we'll run it."

My daughter said, "Yes, Mom. We would love to live in the mountains. And in the winter, it snows up here!"

Then just for fun, we told the agent that we would offer $25,000 less than the asking price. And he said that he would let us know.

100

Well, that same night, when we got home, they called us up to say that the offer had been accepted. And I said to Jorge, "Oh my gosh! How are we going to do it? I don't have any money!"

I'd only offered in jest. I didn't think they would accept that price. But since we didn't jump at the offer, they kept calling, and then they reduced the price by $5,000 more. Now it was $30,000 less than the asking price. Well, then, I told Gloria, Javier, and my son Rafael about that location, and we decided to go look at it again. We all went to see the place. It was a two-hour drive from where we live to the mountains. Well, we all liked it. And my children like to go skiing every year, and it's only ten minutes away from Dodge Ridge, the ski area.

I asked my niece Ana Montanez if she had any money she could lend me for the down payment. They only wanted $20,000 for the business, all the equipment, and the property. The property was one acre of land, and there was an apartment over the restaurant. The apartment was small, but it had all the necessary services. My niece answered that yes she could lend me the money. Well, we made the deal. We had to wait sixty days to finish the escrow. Meanwhile, my son Rafael was going to graduate as a doctor in June 1991. My daughters and I had to get everything ready to give him a party because it was really something special for me.

A Doctor in the Family

There had never been a doctor in my family. I was happy as if I had won the lottery, in spite of all the other bad things that were happening to me because of the divorce. Rafael graduated in San Francisco, California. We all went to his graduation. Afterward, a reporter from the Modesto Bee came to my business because he wanted to know the origins of that young Hispanic who had graduated as a doctor and with honors as an outstanding student. The reporter talked to my son Javier who told him that his mother had raised the children all alone.

Then the reporter told Javier to tell his mother to write the story of how she arrived in this country and said if it was good, they would publish it. Then my son Javier said that I had never gone to school and didn't know how to write in English. The reporter said that I could write in Spanish and then have my bookkeeper translate it to English. They liked the story and they published it in the newspaper.

The day of the party at my house, we had mariachis and food and a lot of guests—all our friends—and we also had television cameras from an American station. Among the guests, there were many Americans and all my employees. More than four hundred people came to my house that day. It was a great day that I will never forget, thank God.

But although I smiled at everybody, there was real pain hidden deep in my heart. What would happen in court? The date was set for July, and they changed it to November. Well, in September of that year, we opened the new business in Cold Springs, the place in the mountains, and we named it La Morenita because that's a name people recognize. That business really helped me a lot. Every weekend I went there with my daughter Erica. The atmosphere, the beautiful green trees, and getting away from the city were all like therapy for me.

Rafael's graduation from Washington University, St. Louis, Missouri, 1986

I had to fight hard to get rid of my love for my husband and accept the reality that he was taking me to court for money. That was nearly impossible for me, but my children were very supportive. My daughter Gloria, her husband, Marcos, and I planned a vacation in November; and we had decided to give a vacation to the employees who had worked for us for a long time, especially because they had never traveled outside the country on vacation. We had decided to go to Cancun, Mexico, for a week in November 1991. But the court date had been set back to November.

Well, what do you think happened? Three days before leaving, I had to go to court. I got there, trembling from head to foot. My son Javier went with me. When we went in, the room was full of people. There was my husband with his lawyer. I felt like I couldn't contain my anger. I wanted to go and hit him and choke him, but at the same time, I thought, *A person who dies doesn't suffer, and he ought to live and pay for all the harm he has done to me.*

There were also a lot of lawyers who knew me because they ate in my restaurant, and the judge did too, and they asked me, "Lupe, what are you doing here? We've never seen you here before."

And I answered, "Well, there's always a first time."

I was praying in my thoughts, begging God not to let the judge tell me that I had to pay the money my husband wanted. It wasn't fair. I had already given him a lot. Well, the moment came to go before the judge, my husband with his lawyer and me with mine. I could hear my husband tell his lawyer, "Tell the judge that she doesn't want to pay me the rest of the money. Tell him to make her pay me."

The two lawyers spoke to the judge, and after a few questions, he said, "I can't do anything. I need more information, and we have to set a new court date. You can all leave now."

Well, that first trip to court and seeing that man again filled me with sadness. Nevertheless, three days later, I went to Cancun with my daughter Erica, Gloria, Javier, the grandchildren, and nine employees. I was so sad there that I even got sick in Cancun, thinking that my husband really didn't know what he was doing. Money had driven him crazy. Where was it all going to end? I had the courage to fight for what was mine, but it was all useless; employees cheered me up a little because they were really happy.

When we got back from vacation, I really felt sick from despair, and the record in my brain was scratched from so much thinking. When my daughter Erica would get home from school, I would say, "Let's go shopping."

I had never gone shopping so much in my whole life, but I couldn't watch television because everything I saw hurt me, and Erica was also in bad shape. She no longer went to see her father. The last time she had gone was on a day her father was giving himself a birthday party, and when she came home, she said to me, "Mommy, I don't want to go back to my father's house. Don't tell me to go."

And I answered, "Honey, he's your father."

And she said, "I'm never going to see him again."

She cried. We both cried. I knew that he would say that I wasn't letting her go to his house.

A Little Justice

Erica didn't even want to go out of the house to ride her bicycle. She came home from school and shut herself in her room. She wasn't doing very well in school either. The teacher sent me a note saying that the child needed help. She had gone to the office and told the principal that she was no longer going to use her father's last name but just Cordoba, her mother's last name. Well, it was a difficult situation. Very difficult. I fought as hard as I could in all directions. I planted a lot of flowers at home, and on weekends, Erica and I went to the mountains to the other business. And we frequently went to the casinos in Reno and to other recreational areas with one of my married daughters and her husband and children. But I was losing all hope of ever freeing myself of the man who was hurting me so much. Since Erica was also suffering, I sought psychological counselling. The doctor helped me and got me a female psychologist for Erica. I started out by taking her once a week the first three months and later once every two weeks.

Well, in February 1992, we had another court date, and once again nothing was settled. Another court date was set. Since I wasn't giving him the money he wanted, he was trying everything he could. Then another court date was set because my husband was saying that I wouldn't let Erica see him. We went to court three times about our daughter. Finally, I had to take the child and the psychologist to court, and her father had to be there so that Erica could tell the psychologist why she didn't want to see him. And that's how he lost the case. He can't see his daughter or even talk to her on the phone.

That's how the year 1992 went, in court and with psychologists and with the lawyers getting as much money out of me as they could. And to top it all off, my lawyer found out he had cancer. I had to find another lawyer because they were going to operate on him and he couldn't work. Getting someone else to take the case meant I had to pay a lot of money. I was too tired! All the profits from the business were going into court dates, lawyers, and psychologists. I had decided that they could put me out on the street, but I wouldn't give anything else to that man. It wasn't fair to pay such a high price for the love of a man fifteen years younger than me.

The night before November 19, 1992, I couldn't sleep because I had decided to really put an end to the divorce proceedings, which had been going on for a year and ten months, without counting four years of pain and suffering. At five o'clock in the morning on that date, I began to think of all the hard years of tremendous work and sacrifice, which didn't seem to mean anything to the lawyers. Pain and suffering don't matter to them. At that instant, I began to cry hard, thinking of how cruel fate had been to me. At that moment, I begged God not to leave me alone. Beside my bed was Erica, my youngest child, the daughter of the man who wrecked my life and hers as well. Erica said, "Mommy, what's the matter? Why are you crying?"

And I answered, "Honey, I can't sleep. But it will go away."

She said, "What's the matter?"

"It's just that when I go to court, I get too nervous. But I'll be okay."

But I cried even harder. I had loved and respected that man too much for him to be doing me so much damage. When I realized I couldn't stop crying, I went to the kitchen and made a cup of tea and smoked a cigarette. That calmed me down. That's when I scribbled what had happened to me that day. Everything is possible with God's help.

That day, we were in court again. Nothing happened. Nothing was settled. They set another date for January 1993. When we left court, my husband's lawyer told me that if I wasn't going to give my husband the money he wanted, he would legally seize everything.

Well, Christmas was about to come, and every year I decorate the house with a lot of Christmas lights. I put up four Christmas trees, and that helped take my mind off my troubles. We get together with our friends every year on December 23, and I make dinner for the employees and their families and children, as well as some clients. Then we shut the restaurant for two days, December 24 and 25, so that everybody can be with their family. Christmas is a season I love, and although we are not a very big family, we are very close. We also like to invite our friends over. Besides, I feel as if all my employees are my family, not just workers. I get along well with them and I love them all. Well, the new year brought good news. The public voted us the best restaurant for Mexican food. Us! La Morenita! They made a book of recipes and they wrote about one of my dishes. It was wonderful. It made me very happy that somebody appreciated what I was doing.

CHAPTER 6

Triumph, Laughter, and Tears

An Invitation

ON JANUARY 8, 1993, MY son Javier was working the night shift at the restaurant, and I was at home. He called me to say that the secretary of Gary Condit, a Californian congressman, had gone to the restaurant to invite me to Washington DC to make some appetizers for a party in honor of President Bill Clinton the day before he was to be sworn in as president. Gary Condit, the congressman, was going to give the party, and they were inviting me. I immediately got annoyed with my son. I said, "What? How can you joke with me like that? I don't like it! Why are you making fun of me?"

And he said, "It's true, Mom. If you don't believe me, I'll leave the phone number here so that you can call him tomorrow because you have to make your reservations." He repeated, "Really, Mom. It's true."

After we hung up, I called Gloria and Esmeralda, and none of us could believe it, but it was true. We talked with Donna, the secretary, and she said that Gary really liked our green salsa and our food and that he wanted us to go to Washington. And I said, "How are we going to cook there? We don't know anybody."

She said, "Just take everything in a freezer chest."

Then Gloria called Washington to talk to her husband Marcos's stepbrother, who was studying in Washington. He said that if we wanted to go, he would pick us up at the airport and help us out when we were there. I'd say the invitation was sent from heaven because I was going through a very difficult time. It lifted my spirits and helped me a lot because I could see that not all people are alike. There are still many good people. Well, Donna made reservations for us at the hotel and paid for the plane tickets. I went with my three daughters. It was an unforgettable trip, full of emotion. On Sunday night, January 19, 1993, we flew there from Sacramento, California.

At President Clinton's inauguration in 1993 in the Capitol Building
(Left to right) Gloria with son Robbie; Esmeralda, Erica,
Carolyn Condit, Lupe, and Congressman Gary Condit

But on the eighteenth, one day earlier, we had to go to court. Can you imagine that? On one hand, a triumph, and on the other, court. But it was all for nothing. They just gave me the divorce, and we still didn't know when everything would end. The judge was in a room with the lawyers, mine and my enemy's. They came out, and he said, "You can leave. I'll let you know when to come back."

And you know what? That time, it didn't hurt me so much to be in court. I guess I was getting used to it. Or maybe I was excited about the trip that I was going to make to Washington. Well, that night, we arrived at the Sacramento airport carrying a large, heavy ice chest. We were bringing everything from my restaurant, even the avocados for the guacamole. We had the chips and paper plates in plastic bags. When we got to the airport, they weighed the ice chest, and then the person in charge of baggage said, "You can't take this. It weighs too much. What are you going to do with all this, anyway?"

We answered, "We're going to make appetizers for a party for President Bill Clinton," and we showed him the invitation.

The baggage man quickly went to talk to another man in the office, and he said to us, "We'll get you a box right away and we'll get rid of some weight by taking out anything extra."

And they arranged everything for us themselves. Do you see what power and politics can do? Well, we arrived in Washington DC, and they treated us like queens. Marcos's brother picked us up at the airport, and we rented a station wagon. That day, they gave us a tour of the city—all the historic buildings, the White House, and the capital. At night, they took us to eat in a beautiful, elegant restaurant. When we got back to the hotel, we had so many phone calls that we couldn't even answer some of them. The people from a radio station—KLOC, Radio Alegria—from Modesto, California, wanted to talk to us via satellite, and the journalists and the secretary of Gary Condit, the congressman who had invited us, really made us feel important. The next day, the twenty-first, we prepared all the food very early in a restaurant loaned to us by an aunt of my son-in-law Marcos's stepbrother. At two in the afternoon, we had an appointment at the capital.

When we got to Gary's office, the journalists were there, asking us questions about how we brought all the food from California and what we were going to serve at the dinner. After they interviewed us, a group of people took us on a tour of the whole capital building, including the conference rooms and the banquet room all decorated with a lot of fresh plants, where we were going to serve the appetizers. The table where we were going to serve the food was decorated in Mexican style.

Well, that was a really exciting night, with journalists and television cameras all over the place. I had never seen so many people all together or so many security officers as there were for the inauguration in my whole life. There was a big parade and a lot of parties in honor of President Clinton. They gave us passes for the formal party and for the President's speech. You'd have to see it to believe it! They also interviewed us on an international television channel, and we were seen on television in Mexico. Besides, we took our own film and a lot of pictures.

There at the party, we ran into a longtime friend, Richard Patterson, a councilman from the city of Modesto, California. When he saw us, he was so happy that he embraced us and called us his "sisters." Well, when we got back to California, all of our friends and restaurant clients were so excited that you'd think we had gone to the moon. All my neighbors had saved the newspaper for us. We came out in the newspaper in three cities. Later, in March of the same year, 1993, Carolina Vernal, a television reporter from KCSO, Channel 19 of Modesto, called me to make a date to interview me at home for her show, *Our Community*. After interviewing me, she said my story was very interesting and that she was also going to interview all my children. And she did. When she finished all the interviews, an hour-long video was made and shown several times on Channel 19, Univision in Modesto and cable television chains in this area. It was great publicity for my business, and it encouraged the community as well.

It cheered me up, too, because the divorce situation had really ruined me both internally and economically. Well, that interview with Carolina and the invitation to Washington made me stronger than ever. I learned to live alone, without a man, keeping my mind occupied with my daughter Erica and my business. I was always thinking about doing new things in my house as well as my business.

My Treasure

Finally, in July 1993, the court case was over. My ex-husband no longer had any lawyers who would help him, and he felt lost. He went to speak to my lawyer, saying that instead of $80,000, he would settle for $25,000; but I said no. Afterward, my lawyer charged me for those visits, and that outraged me. I was almost on the point of fighting with my lawyer over that. But my children said, "Mom, you've got to get this over with. Offer him $15,000 and get this nightmare over with once and for all."

I called my lawyer and said that I would offer him $15,000 and that if he didn't want it, then the judge could decide. But if it were up to the judge, we would have to be in court for who knows how long, and I was really fed up with court and with throwing my good money after bad, as they say. Well, my ex-husband accepted the $15,000, and that's how the two and a half years of nightmares in court ended in July 1993.

I guess I'll never know the reason why that man did all that to me. I keep asking myself how anybody could be so cold-hearted. Money isn't everything in life, only a part of it. As you can see, the price I paid was way too high for the love of a man who was fifteen years younger than I. But it was the best lesson life could give me. I have learned to be happy without a man's love. It's enough to have the love of my children and my grandchildren, of which I now have eight. And although the divorce was horrible, I have my treasure, my daughter Erica, whom I wouldn't give up for anything in the world. God has always taken care of us, and I always thank Him. That was the best lesson of my life. I know that solitude is not a good companion. It's very important to have a man in the house, but since finding the right man has been impossible for me, I have adapted to life without a man's presence and love. Although it's not easy, I'm learning how to do it.

My grandchildren from Esmeralda's marriage are Chastity, Nicole, Ezekiel, and Zeph. My grandchildren from Gloria's marriage are Brityn, Hillary, Jordan, and Roberto. I don't quarrel with my sons-in-law or with my daughters-in-law. I don't meddle in their lives. I love them all a lot.

For me, my family comes first. I accept their good points and their bad ones because nobody is perfect, and I am the last person to judge the errors of others.

The American Dream

In February 1994, a daughter of my sister Alvina, who lives in Palo Alto, California, told me they were selling the restaurant where she was working. She asked if I wanted to buy it. She'd been working there for ten years. Aurora said to me, "Auntie, buy it. My husband Miguel and I will run it. If not, we'll be out of work."

Well, I knew she was a very good worker, and besides, she knew how to prepare the recipes that I use in my business. I talked about it with my daughters, and we went to Palo Alto to see the place. The restaurant was in a very good area with lots of business and very close to downtown. We really like it and we went to talk to the owner. The price was very reasonable. We only had to fix up a few things and brighten it up, which isn't hard for me. Well, after getting some information and talking to my niece and her husband, we went back about three times and thought about the changes we would make in the kitchen because they served American food there and we were going to serve Mexican food. We made the deal, and the place would be ours on May 1.

(Left to right) Nicole, Ezekiel, Chasity, Esmeralda, George, and Zeph

That was in February 1994. In the first week of March, a man who worked for a real estate agency came to my restaurant at lunch hour. We were very full and had a lot of people waiting for tables. I was working as the cashier and receptionist. And when I put his name on the waiting list, he asked, "Lupe, wouldn't you like to see a place I'm selling?"

He'd been telling me for about three months that there was a very big, pretty restaurant for sale. It was about twenty-five minutes away from my location. So one day, I sent a manager to see the place, and he told me that it was incredible because it was very big and had very good equipment. But I thought they wanted too much money, so I said I wasn't interested. "Lupe, please go see the place," the agent said. "If you don't like it, I won't mention it again."

I answered him, "How much do you want for everything?"

He said, "I'm going to give it to you, free."

I answered, laughing, "That's not true. You're not going to give it to me for nothing! Tell me how much so I can get interested in going to see it."

And he answered, "I won't tell you until you see if you like it. Look how many customers you have, and you don't want to see the place I'm offering?"

Well, since he insisted so much, I made an appointment that day. But I didn't keep the appointment because I had something else to do and I didn't have his phone number. But he called me right away and said, "What happened, Lupe? I was waiting for you and you never came."

I told him I hadn't been able to go, and we made another appointment. Just then, my daughter Gloria came to my house, and I told her that the man wanted me to go see a restaurant and that he was going to give it to me. I asked her, "Do you believe that? I don't want any more responsibility. I have too much already."

And she answered, "Mom, let's go see it. There's nothing to lose."

Then I said yes, and that same day, Gloria and I went to see the place. Well, we couldn't believe it. We were really surprised. From there, we called Marcos, Gloria's husband, to come see the place. The price and the quality of the equipment were incredible. That's because the person who owned the restaurant had a heart attack, and the business failed and the bank took it over, and they were selling it off at an incredible price. Everything was completely new. There was seating for 150 people and there was a beautifully set-up bar. Gloria said, "Mom, buy it. The two of us can handle it. Marcos and I will manage it. You don't have to worry about anything. Just help us train the cooks."

Well, you're not going to believe it. They checked my income tax returns, and in two days, the place was ours. I had very good credit, so there was no problem. But we already had paid for some plane tickets and we had reservations to go to Disney World in Orlando, Florida, for a week's vacation. Two days before we left, Gloria and I got all the permits and applied for a liquor license. How were we going to decorate it? They only thing it didn't have was the cookware. When we got back, the first thing we did was to buy the pots.

Well, it was the first time we had opened such a large restaurant. Although I had a lot of experience when all the pots and all the merchandise arrived, I said to myself, "It's really going to be a big challenge to get everything in place!"

There was a lot of work to do, but we attacked it energetically, and in three weeks, we opened. People were so excited that I could hardly believe it. That's because when we bought the place, we put up some huge signs saying La Morenita was going to open a branch, but we didn't say when. During those three weeks, a lot of people called us, some to ask for work and others to find out when we were opening and still others to sell things. The phone was ringing all day long. It was hard to believe!

We didn't want to advertise or have a grand opening until three weeks after we opened in order to train all the employees well. But even so, we hardly put up the Open sign and the place was full, thank heavens. But we really had to work hard. At first, we had a lot of workers, but in a new place, one always feels lost. On the Cinco de Mayo, we held our grand opening. We had a traditional mariachi band. That day, we received a lot of presents and congratulatory hugs and kisses. I was in the kitchen with the cooks, and the clients came in there to congratulate me. All the Chamber of Commerce members arrived with their ribbon and their big scissors to welcome us. How can I ever forget the marvelous things our clients did?

Then reporters from the Modesto Bee came to interview us two months after we opened. When the article came out, it was great publicity for us. They included a color photo of Gloria and me with that interview. The bank where I have my accounts even put the newspaper clipping up so everybody could see it and read it. It was a whole page! Well, money comes and goes, but the love that people give us stays with us forever. We will never forget it.

Now let me tell you about the restaurant in Palo Alto, California. After working so hard to open in Modesto, I swear I didn't want to open another restaurant just two months later! But what could I do? I already had signed the contract and I didn't want to leave my niece and nephew-in-law unemployed. They were hopeful and happy because they were going to have their jobs assured. And besides, we're partners. They're also owners of the business. How could I disillusion them? I had to do it. Well, my son Javier rented an apartment and moved to Palo Alto to train the waiters, and I trained the cooks. My niece Aurora knew how to prepare my recipes, but she hadn't done it for a long time and she didn't feel very secure. So I was going back and forth two times a week before I could leave them on their own.

Palo Alto is a very big city because many cities come together there. Several people asked me why I was going to open a Mexican restaurant when there were already so many restaurants of all kinds, not to mention bankrupt businesses. They said the reason the man sold me the place in Palo Alto because he had no business. But I answered that my food was different. They said, "All Mexican food is the same."

Then I said to them, "I won't lose by trying."

Well, as usual, we didn't advertise until the cooks had more practice. But God had never forgotten us. Even though we didn't advertise, people came. My son Javier is like a newspaper. People really love him and follow him, so the place filled up, even though we weren't known there. We had no problem getting customers. We opened at the end of May. My son Javier was getting married June 17 to Stephanie, an American girl, and I had to prepare for the wedding because that's the way it's done. How could I leave him to do it alone?

Javier's Wedding

That wedding was very different from those of my daughters or any other that I was accustomed to. Stephanie's parents and I stood at the door, greeting all the guests. I was accustomed to greeting the guests but not so formally. And this time, I got a lot of hugs and congratulations. People were very kind and sentimental about the way my family stayed close and had gotten ahead, not only personally but also professionally. During the reception, my son Rafael made a speech remembering everything from all the mischief the kids had gotten into together to the way Javier had contributed to helping the business grow. The food, the mariachi, the happiness, and the emotion all contributed to those unforgettable moments.

So in three months, I opened two businesses and prepared a large wedding. That time, I really could hardly stand so many emotions all at once. Javier went on his honeymoon after the reception.

Erica's Fifteenth Birthday

I don't know how, but time sure flies! By now, it was only three months until my daughter Erica would be fifteen years old. I had dreamed about giving her a big party and buying her a beautiful dress and thought that she would have maids of honor and their escorts, which is the Mexican tradition. But when I talked to her about celebrating, she didn't know if she really wanted a party. Then she looked at a magazine with dresses for quinceañera parties. We saw a lot of very pretty dresses, but she didn't like any of them. My daughter Gloria and I said that if she didn't want a party, then we would celebrate the birthday by taking a vacation, and Erica wanted to go to Hawaii. And Gloria said that she would also like to see Hawaii, so we went to a travel agent and made reservations for Gloria, her husband, her four children, and me.

But about a month before the trip, Gloria found a house for sale close to where I live. She liked it so much she decided not to go on vacation. She preferred buying the house, so we canceled the reservations because Erica and I didn't want to go alone. By then, it was too late to plan a big party, so it looked like there would be no party and no vacation. Well, it was only a week until Erica's fifteenth birthday on November 14, 1995, and I was feeling a little sad because I wasn't doing anything for her. Then I spoke to Gloria and my other daughter, Esmeralda, and I told them how I felt about not doing anything for Erica's birthday because you're only fifteen once in your life. Then Gloria said, "Let's go out for breakfast and talk about what we can do."

Well, that very day, I put my mind to work at a hundred miles an hour, and we decided to give her a surprise party. Her birthday was on Tuesday, so she would be in school. At breakfast, Gloria told me that she would help rent the tables and chairs and decorate all the tables and that I should be in charge of the meal and of inviting all my friends and relatives. I also had to find a mariachi because a party without music isn't a party. Besides, mariachi music is my favorite, and I think it can even wake up the dead! Well, I had good luck in getting the mariachi because it was for a Tuesday and not the weekend, so they had no other commitments.

Lupe and Erica on a cruise to the Caribbean, 1997

I started to work really fast but without letting her suspect anything. I keep all my Christmas lights until they no longer work. I decorated all the front of the house with white Christmas lights. I set all my trees out in front of the house. I didn't think Erica would see the lights, but she did and she asked, "Why did you put up the Christmas lights so soon?"

I answered, "Because it's such good weather, so now I won't have to put them up when it gets colder," and she believed me.

Well, I told my many restaurant employees that they were all invited. I made the invitations by phone. And another friend, Jose Luis Arias, made me a beautiful banner to put at the entrance of the house and he came to put it up. Then I decided to get a limousine to pick up Erica from school. I asked one of my workers, Jaime Herrera, if he could get the limousine. "With pleasure. It will be my gift to your daughter," he said.

Now there were only three days to go. Then I said to Erica, "I didn't make a big party for you the way I wanted to, but I'm going to have a dinner for you and you can invite your friends and schoolmates. I want you to invite eight of them to come home from school with you."

I told her that my son Javier would pick them up in his station wagon and take them all to get ice cream. And I also told Erica that I wanted us to go buy her a dress because at least for her birthday, she should go to school in a dress. Well, we went to the mall to buy the dress. We were there for hours and hours, and she didn't like a single dress. I saw a lot of very pretty dresses for her, but she didn't like any of them. Finally, instead of a dress, she bought a long skirt and a blouse. What can you do? I didn't want her to know that I was planning a surprise for her.

I called up my son Rafael, the doctor. He lives in Colorado. I asked if he could come to Erica's birthday party, and even though he was very busy, he said he would come but could only stay with us as long as the party lasted.

Well, the day arrived. When Erica got up, I gave her a big hug and spanked her bottom fifteen times, and she went to school. Because I was so excited about the surprise I was going to give her,

I didn't even realize that she hadn't put on the clothes I had bought her. So she went to school in her Levi's. I didn't notice it until she got out of the car.

After I left her at school, I spent the whole day cooking, and Gloria and another friend fixed up the tables and blew up a lot of balloons and put flowers on all the tables. We set everything up outside in front of the garage, in the garage, and around the pool. On one side of the garage, we put a big table covered with tablecloths and set it up for a buffet. I cooked a lot of tamales and pozole and traditional atole and salsa, chips, tostadas, guacamole, chicken taquitos, rolls, and a huge cake.

Well, when my daughter Erica left school and her friends saw a limousine parked outside of the school, they said, "Look at that! What a limousine!"

One of her friends said, "Erica, it's for you."

And she answered, "What makes you think it's here for me?'

At that moment, the chauffeur got out and said, "Erica Cordoba?"

They were all shouting excitedly. Then my son Javier got there and took them on excursion to the city of Modesto, California. He took them to a mall and bought them sodas and then took them in the limousine to one of my bigger restaurants. He had them get out there to be serenaded with "Las Mañanitas." All of the workers came out to sing to them and used pots and spoons to make music. But Erica still didn't know about the real surprise. I had told my son Javier not to the bring them home until 5:00 p.m. That way, when they got to the house, all the guests were already there, all the lights were lit, and the mariachi was ready to play "Las Mañanitas."

They arrived and Erica was so excited and emotional that tears rolled down her cheeks. All the girls had their school backpacks in the limousine, and they were all really surprised and excited. They couldn't believe it. It was unforgettable. My daughter and the other girls even danced in the street to the mariachi music. I think that sometimes things come out better when you don't plan them too much. You only have to put your mind to work, as well as your body.

Rafael's Wedding

Soon after that, my son Rafael was engaged to his girlfriend, and they were going to get married on August 30, 1996. His fiancée was an American girl who is a clinical nutritionist from W. Virginia. Rafael is pretty special. He doesn't like extravagance; he prefers things more formal. He doesn't like to show off. Thank heavens I like the way he is! Well, those two planned their wedding well in advance, and this time, I didn't have to cook or do any of the work. They and the girl's family did everything. I just helped out with a little money.

At Rafael's wedding with Grandfather Jose, Rafael, and Lupe

We made our reservations early because the whole family was going to Denver, Colorado, and we could only be there four days because we can't all leave the business at the same time. We took two of our employees, Jaime and Marta. They've been working for us for many years, and my son holds them in high esteem. We also took another friend, Adolfo Ramirez, who was going to take the video of the wedding, and Robert and Norma Smallwood, the parents of my son-in-law Marcos. Robert was almost like a second father for my children. He gave them a lot of good advice when they were children. I would have liked to take all my employees, but it was impossible without closing all our restaurants. Besides, it was very far away.

Well, that wedding was really special because there were parties for three days. In the invitations, my son Rafael had included a map showing where each celebration would take place. The first day, Thursday, August 29, they had rented a house near a very high mountain. They had a barbecue there for both families and all the relatives. The served some delicious chicken and a kind of rice I had never eaten before and lots of side dishes like fruit salad, vegetables, and a lot of other things, as well as things to drink.

The only person we knew was Elizabeth, my son's bride-to-be. We didn't know anyone in her family. That day, we met her whole family, and they were so nice that we felt as if we'd known them for a long time. We didn't feel like strangers for a minute. There was a lot of communication. That afternoon, you could feel the sincerity, love, and joy of everybody gathered there. I told my son Rafael that I wasn't going to cry during his wedding because it was bad luck, and he just laughed. Well, about 10:30 p.m., we saw two gigantic limousines arrive. They were going to take Rafael and all his friends to a bachelor party in a nightclub.

That night, a group of us decided to get together the next morning for a trip up the mountain. It's really high and has an interesting history. Well, that's what we did. We met the next day and went with a guide who explained the history of the mountain to us. About forty people went, including the bride, the groom, and Elizabeth's grandfather, who was eighty-four years old at the time. When I asked Elizabeth if her grandfather was going, she said he was. I wondered how he would be able to climb up such a high mountain!

Well, believe it or not, he climbed up and went down as easy as can be. If I remember right, the round trip was eight miles. That was on August 29. That same evening, there was a dinner held in a banquet hall for both families and all those who were taking part in the wedding. They served Italian food, and of course, it was delicious. They had people there in uniform serving all kinds of drinks and appetizers. They even had a microphone so people could talk about the bride and groom, telling things they had done when they were very young. I asked my daughter Gloria to talk about something beautiful that my son Rafael did when he was only eight years old. On Mother's Day, his gift to me was to get up before me, very early, and go to the kitchen. He made me breakfast and brought it to me in bed. At that time, we really didn't have any money. That memory brought tears to my eyes.

My mind went back to the hard, difficult times we had gone through, but I made a huge effort to hold in my tears. It was a happy night after all. All the adults left at about 10:30 p.m. to go to a nightclub where those who wanted to could dance or play pool. What impressed me the most was seeing that all the guests went along, and the majority of them were doctors with their wives, aunts and uncles, and brothers and sisters. We left the club at about 1:30 a.m.

The next day was the main event. We had to be in church at noon. Well, that day, the local team was playing a very important football game in Boulder, near Denver. The majority of the athletes were staying at the same hotel where we were. It was a huge hotel with a lot of tennis courts and areas for other sports. There was traffic for miles around and there was no place to park, but they were going to send a limousine to take us to church. Well, because the traffic was so awful, it got to be time for us to go and the limousine hadn't arrived, and we were outside the hotel, worried because we were going to arrive late. Right then, a limousine arrived. We thought it was the one that was coming for us, but it turned out that it had brought some athletes. Then a woman who was with them asked us where we were going and what we were waiting for. My daughter Esmeralda answered, "We're late getting to church for my brother's wedding."

The lady said, "The traffic's terrible. Why don't you go in this limousine? After all, it's already paid for."

Well, that's what we did. It took us to church, and the problem was solved. My son knew about the game in advance, and do you know what he did? He rented a double decker bus to go and pick up the guests from the hotel where they were staying because there really was no place to park cars. After the photographers were finished with us, I went to the room where the bride and the bridesmaids were getting ready. And just then, the woman in charge of the ceremony said, "It's time to go in."

At the door to the church, I saw a friend of my son and Elizabeth's with Rafael's two little dogs. He loves them as if they were really his children. They really are darling. They're tiny and white. They brought them to church and decorated them with colored paper collars. Well, you won't believe it, but just seeing them made me so emotional that I couldn't stop my tears. How did they think of even this little detail? The doggies are so cute and well mannered. They took videos of the bride and groom, with the dogs in their arms, outside of the church.

Well, there was a traditional mariachi playing Mexican songs outside of the church, even though there were only fourteen Mexican guests and three Puerto Rican guests. All the rest were from the US. The bus took all of the guests and us, too, from church. It had to make two trips. We went to a restaurant where we ate appetizers and pizza and had drinks and danced to mariachi music until about four o'clock in the afternoon.

Seeing all of the Americans with us dancing to Mexican music really made me feel sentimental. It was also very exciting to see so many doctor friends who had come from different places to be there for my son. I'm not bragging, but it was exciting for me to be introduced to all the people who were together at the university in St. Louis, Missouri, and coworkers in the San Francisco hospital and friends from New York, Chicago, Palo Alto, California, and even from Australia. Families and friends came from Oakland, California, and even from Australia. My son is a doctor; Elizabeth, her father, and her father's brothers are all doctors; even her grandfather is a doctor. The majority of the guests were doctors, and they were all so pleasant and happy! They loved the mariachi, and everybody danced to everything, even the "Macarena." The party went on. We finally left when the mariachi couldn't play any longer because they had another commitment.

Then we all walked about five or six blocks through the city to the place where the formal dinner was ready for us, with dancing and a full-service open bar so that guests could drink whatever they wanted. After the dinner, they used a projector to show pictures of the two families in their happiest moments. Elizabeth's father spoke, and the eighty-four-year-old grandfather prayed for God's blessings for the happiness of the bride and the groom. Then the dance started, and we all enjoyed it to the maximum.

I think I was most surprised by how well organized everything was, because in general, something goes wrong at a wedding. Well, by the end of the night, the bridal couple seemed like two robots. They'd been on foot all day and night, talking to the guests and grinning from ear to ear. They danced until the end of the dance. A lot of the guests were staying in the hotel where the reception took place, but we weren't. A taxi took us back to our hotel.

Farewells aren't always pleasant, but everything was over, and the next day, we would go back to Turlock. We got back to the hotel and slept. I slept about two hours and then I began to think about the wedding. Thank heavens everything had turned out well. It was really special, different from the other weddings we had had in our family. The bitter times of my life popped into my mind, and without warning, tears poured out and I couldn't stop crying. I had to go into the bathroom and I still couldn't stop crying. That day, all the way home, the tears kept sneaking up on me. I said to my daughters. "What's going on with me? I didn't cry during the wedding, and now I can't stop. I told Rafael I wasn't going to cry at his wedding, so why am I getting so sentimental now?"

Well, about three weeks before my son's wedding, I had had a terrible dream that the wedding was a disaster. I dreamed that my son jilted the bride because somebody wrote him a letter saying horrible things about her. I dreamed that the hotel we were staying in was destroyed, with the floors all up in the air and the walls falling down, and we couldn't find the dresses we were going to wear to the wedding. When I dreamed, I saw my son taking off his clothes because he wasn't going to get married, and I cried disconsolately until my daughter Erica woke me up. I quickly told her what I was dreaming and I talked to my other daughter, Gloria, and told her about my terrible nightmare. But I was sure that it wouldn't turn out to be true. I said to myself, "This time, it will come out exactly the opposite of what I dreamed of."

Well, Gloria didn't keep the secret, and she told my son Rafael about my nightmare about his wedding. Since my son knows that many of my good and bad dreams have come true, he got curious and called me up immediately. I wasn't home, and he left a message on my machine saying that he wanted to know everything I had dreamed. Talk about the power of suggestion! Then I returned his call and told him all about the dream and said, "This won't turn out to be true. It's going to be exactly the opposite. Your wedding will be really special because you are really special. Don't worry, just forget it. Bad dreams have to turn into good ones."

We have to change, or try to change, bad things into good ones. It doesn't matter what it is. The mind has so much power, and I can't imagine why some people don't believe that. We let ourselves get dragged down by the romantic and professional entanglements we get into. You have to fight and fight and never forget that through perseverance comes triumph and that after darkness there is light if we let it in. A lot of people think that they have to study and pursue a career but that if they have a profession but don't speak English, they still can't get anywhere. Excuse me, that's not exactly true. Anybody, male or female, who wants to be somebody in life, can indeed do it with God's help. I know that studying is very important, but it's much more important to want to work and get ahead and to respect one's fellowman. You have to be honest with yourself. That's the most important thing in anybody's life.

Rafael and Elizabeth, 1996

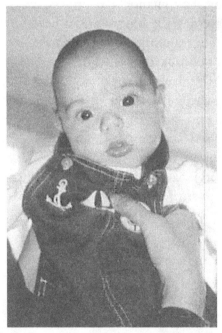

Rafael's firstborn son, Michael, born November 1997

CHAPTER 7

Epilogue

I'M STILL IN CHARGE OF the restaurant in Palo Alto and also the one in Ceres, but now I'm not alone. My daughter Esmeralda and her husband, Jorge, help me to run the one in Ceres, although I'm still the administrator. Well, two months after we opened the Palo Alto restaurant, we had a grand opening with three hours of mariachi music for our new customers. That day, we had lines of people waiting for tables. I was so happy that all the work didn't even make me tired! I, who arrived in this country with three children and without a cent in my purse, without a house or a job, with absolutely nothing, had finally made it. I really had to write a book to tell you how I grew, step by step, working hard to make my dreams come true.

I'm really proud of the fact that I was able to do it honestly. I didn't have to sell drugs or my body to get ahead, and my children were able to prepare themselves professionally. Those who chose not to study work in my restaurants and help run them, and they can all have a much better future because of the things I went through. Everything that's mine is theirs as well. And with all the great sacrifices I made, not only my family and I have benefited from the recipes I invented for Mexican food but also many other families. Those recipes weren't previously in the San Joaquin Valley. Many of my workers learned how to cook for me and then went out to open more restaurants with the same recipes; they changed the numbers on the menus but they're the same recipes. They also give their restaurants different names, and to attract clients, many of those who have opened new places tell their customers that we are the same owners.

What do you think of that? They've never paid me for using my recipes. Right now, there are nineteen restaurants that serve food and salsas made with my own recipes, but it hasn't hurt my business at all! Some of them even advertised in the newspaper that I had given them La Morenita's menu, and on the day their ad appeared in the newspaper, they could hardly handle so many people, even though they had almost no customers before.

Well, even though love can hurt us, it's still the most beautiful thing in the world. It gives us life; it gives us joy. I'm talking about love in general—love for parents, for children, between a husband and a wife, for friends, for our home, for the work we do. If we don't love ourselves or have high self-esteem, it's very difficult to leave poverty behind and lift ourselves up again after each failure we may have. One must have a lot of faith in God and also in oneself. Nobody is going to help us if we don't help ourselves.

I have suffered a lot for love and not just from the men I have loved but also from friends that I have loved a lot and who have somehow deceived me or taken advantage of me. That hurts me a lot too.

I think that a person who has never known real love probably either doesn't suffer, or else lives a bitter life, sad and withdrawn from everything because he or she doesn't want to suffer. But I don't think that's a real life. We have to understand that nobody is free of problems. And absolutely nobody is perfect. Anybody who claims to be perfect is lying. We always make some mistakes, big or small. Besides, we're only going to live once. To live eternally unhappy isn't fair. We ought to look for a way to be happy, even just a little bit. And how can we be happy? By giving love to those around us. It's the only way.

Life has given me many experiences, good and bad. You may say I was lucky to have good children. And yes, thank God, they really are good. But they also made mistakes and they made me cry who knows how many times. But since I never thought I was perfect, I had to help them through the difficult times of adolescence, and I would never have been able to kick them out of the house. Why? Because that's not the way to help them. I still remember when my son Rafael was in high school, I bought a pickup truck for the business, and my son Rafael drove it. Well, when he went to St. Louis, Missouri, to study at the university, the pickup looked like a circus car—dented all over. The doors were pushed in, the rear bumper was dented, and so was the one in front. The sides of the car looked as if it had been wrecked in an automobile race. Then my other son, Javier, was always getting tickets for driving at high speeds. But he was never involved in fights or drugs, and that makes me very happy. They also respect others and they really love people and our customers. If they weren't like that, we would never have been able to come so far.

Like me, they have a lot of friends, rich and poor. For us, everybody has the same worth, whether they be children, adults, or very old people. We don't look at colors or nationalities. Everyone is welcome in our businesses.

My Thoughts

I'd also like to tell you about what I think now after so many failures and successes and about all the experiences life has given me. I thank God for giving me the strength and the intelligence to fight hard day and night, although there's still a lot left for me to do.

I think work is the best medicine for one's health. Think about being in a house with nothing to do. How boring must that be? The body and the brain need exercise. It's possible that a housewife who has a lot of children works all day, day after day, a really tiresome daily routine with no income. But if that woman would look for a part-time job doing something she likes to do, I am sure she would feel much better and would have a clearer mind. For example, when my mind can't keep up with all the details of the business, I go someplace for a day or two or on a vacation, even though it's just a week twice a year, and that's how I can keep things going. We have to think of new things to do, even if they are just little things, and that will help us.

My Dreams

I'm going to tell you about my dreams when I'm sleeping. I'm almost sure that I have one waking life and another when I'm asleep. When I'm asleep, my mind tells me about what's to come and it warns me because I have previously dreamed many things that have happened to me later. Sometimes the dreams come two or three years before the event. But one way or another, they become reality. When I married the first time, I dreamed of being in a foreign country and that I didn't understand anything the people were taking about. In my dream, I asked, "Why did I leave my country?"

I can't remember how many times I had that dream and I would say to my friends, "Why do I dream about being in a foreign country and about not being able to understand what people are saying?"

And they would say to me, "Oh, Lupe! They're just nightmares!"

And when I came to the United States, I really didn't understand any English. And before that, I had never even thought that I might come to California. Afterward, I dreamed that my husband would leave us, and I cried a lot in the dream because I had no place to live and no money for anything. And when I woke up, I asked, "Why am I having such horrible dreams?"

Later, everything I had dreamed did happen. It all came true. As the years passed, I began to dream about a checkbook with a lot of pale blue checks. And in the dream I thought, *But I have no have money in the bank in order to write those checks.*

At that time, the only thing I had was my children. The money I earned was barely enough to buy food, and I wasn't even thinking about ever opening a checking account. But that also happened as time passed. And when my son Rafael was young, he always told me that he was going to study medicine and be a doctor. And I dreamed that I was there when he graduated as a doctor. I said to myself when I woke up, "Well, I actually liked that dream!"

When we were very poor, I often dreamed of being in really pretty places on vacations and cruises. I would think about it and tell my daughters, "Well, here we are with nothing, and I'm dreaming about being on cruises. I've never been on a boat, and I'm dreaming about being on vacation on one."

I would even laugh about it. After I started the business, I dreamed about having the restaurant completely full with people waiting in line. Then we couldn't make enough food, and I would tell the helpers, "Do you believe what I dreamed about? That we couldn't handle so many people. That there was a line of people waiting for tables."

And we would laugh. At that time, we did have customers, but there was never a line. We could manage with just one cook and a helper. I cooked alone. But that dream also became reality. Now, thank God, there are three cooks and a helper on each shift. Sometimes I really don't believe it!

I also dreamed about marrying again and having a little brunette girl with fat little hands. And I would say, "Get married again? I'd have to be crazy!"

Well, crazy or not, I got married again and had my daughter Erica, just as I had dreamed. After I sold my first house and I was married for the second time, I began to dream about a prettier one—a two-story house with a swimming pool and gardens in front and in back. But I never saw a house anywhere designed like the one in my dreams. I dreamed about the same house three times, and the last time I dreamed about it, I was decorating it with Christmas lights. I would say to my husband, "Why am I dreaming about that house? I'm not even thinking about moving. I really like this house, and it has everything I need."

Well, I don't know how such things happen, but I changed my mind, and one day, we built the house exactly the way I saw it in my dreams. But at the same time I was dreaming about the house, I was also dreaming that my husband would leave me and go off with another woman. And I dreamed about being in court, and I cried a lot as I dreamed. Sometimes he would wake me up and ask, "What's the matter? Why are you crying?"

And I would answer, "Oh, I have really terrible nightmares! God willing, they'll never come true!"

At that time, we were very happy. At least, I was. I begged God not to let that dream come true because I didn't want it to be true for anything in the world. But it also turned out to be true and even worse that I had dreamed.

Afterward, I also began to dream that I was opening another Mexican restaurant on a high mountain surrounded by pretty green pine trees. I began to think, *This dream is really crazy. As if I would open a restaurant on a mountain! What nonsense!*

I told my workers about it, and as always, we laughed. I said, "Silly dreams!"

Well, I don't know how and I hardly believe it, but an opportunity arose, and it also became a reality. I opened that business high up in the mountains, and I even had a playground built so children could play there. And then I began to dream new dreams about having a very big beautiful restaurant. I dreamed about it being full of customers, and then my dreams began to worry me. I always told my daughters about them. That time, I said to them, "This couldn't possibly be true."

Esmeralda said to me, "Oh, Mom! You and your dreams!"

And I also dreamed several times about being on television. I said to myself, "Really, Lupe, you're either going crazy or you have two lives, one when you're awake and another when you're asleep."

And I dreamed about the same restaurant again, and it was only twenty-five minutes away from the one in Ceres. And I would wake up and say, "How am I going to open another restaurant? Business is so hard these days!"

As I told you earlier, I opened that pretty new restaurant, and it seats 150 people, and we often have a line of people waiting for tables. And to think they almost gave it away to get me to buy it! Not only that, but there's also another one in Palo Alto, two hours away from where I live. And I was on television, not once but several times. I'm still waiting to see if another very clear dream comes true. I've dreamed three times that I won the lottery, and it was the same amount in each dream. I hope that when this book is published, an expert who knows about such things will explain how I dream about what's going to happen in my life. Well, these are a few of the many dreams that have become reality—the biggest ones.

Family

Now I'll tell you what has happened as the years passed, some of the customs my parents had on the ranch where I was born and in that little settlement in Mexico that I'll never forget.

Just on my mother's side of the family, I have sixty-five cousins, the children of my mother's brothers and sisters. They each had more than a dozen children. They were a very happy, close-knit family. Now I ask myself, what happened to all that wonderful family love?

We began to come to the United States, and all that family unity began to come apart. I have a lot of relatives that I hardly know, and some of them live only ten miles away! We all are so involved in work and responsibilities that we forget about our relatives. And that beautiful love unravels. The only times we get together is when a relative dies—that is, if they let me know—and if not, then we don't see one another.

I don't know my relatives on my father's side because I've been in California for thirty years and I really haven't seen them again, except when I go to Mexico; even then, I only see a few of them, and they don't even live in the same area. The majority are in the United States. What happened with my parents' families is the same thing that happened to the families of the men I married.

Our Opportunities

California is the land of opportunities. The only people who don't get ahead are those who don't work. But there is another secret a lot of people don't know, which is that it's more work to use one's money wisely than to earn it. A person can earn a lot of money, but without knowing how to use it wisely, it's going to be difficult to ever stop working. And in spite of all the opportunities there are in California, thousands of families have separated. People have forgotten their parents, their children, and their wives. It's really a pity that they are suffering. Those people prefer to suffer instead of repenting for what they do. There are a lot of people in the world who, when somebody does something good for them, repay that person by trading real love for passing fancies and less decent forms of amusement. One can do whatever one wants, except forget one's parents and children.

It's really a pity that we don't know how to appreciate the good things God gives us. Many people throw them out like garbage without thinking. Nobody can change certain people even advantage as possible, and if they can destroy the other person, they do it. That's the payment they give, and that's the truth. But what do we get out of doing harm to a fellowman? I don't think that ever brings happiness to anybody. If a person really wants to be bad, I'm sure that he or she does the greatest damage to his or her own self. I don't think anybody can be happy over the damage he has done to another person. One way or another, he's going to be punished. I don't want anybody to be offended. I say it because of the experience I have had.

But I also know about true love, without expecting anything in return, and I believe that when we love somebody with no strings attached, we ought to think a little with our head and not just with our heart because unrequited love hurts too much. And I'm talking about love in general. Well, that's what I think now and what I've always thought since I was a little girl.

Hopeless Causes

Now I'd like to tell you about the things that outrage me, which almost make me sick because I can't do anything about them. Even the government, with all its power, can't control them. First, sexual abuse of children. I love children so much. How can people be so cruel? How can they have the heart to abuse an innocent child and destroy a life? I think such people are worse than animals! It makes me sick. And every day, you hear about abuse. It's so horrible there are no words to describe it! Another thing that makes me mad is when the government here in California gives food stamps to poor people on welfare, and some of them sell the stamps to buy liquor or drugs. I know because they've offered me the stamps.

Other things I hate with all my heart are treachery and deception. I prefer to live alone than to share the man I love with another woman. I can't stand it, not even when I see it in another person who has nothing to do with me. Another thing that makes me angry is when I see people treating a child badly, hitting him as if he were not a living being or cursing at him. That really makes me mad. I've seen men and women who are in a bad mood take it all out on the poor little kids. How can they treat their own children that way? What I have begun to think is that parents who treat their children badly were mistreated themselves when they were children. I thank God that I wasn't that way with my children because I hate evil and violence.

Another thing that bothers me is messiness. When I get home, even when I'm really tired from work, I don't rest until I've picked up and cleaned the house a little. It's the same in my restaurants. When I go to any of them, the first thing I see are the things that are out of place. And right away I have to tell people to arrange them right so I can feel at ease. It's just that messiness makes me nervous.

Thoughts about My First Husband

Well, you're probably wondering what happened to my first husband, Eduardo, the one who abandoned me. Nine years after he left us, he sent his children some money so they could go to see him in San Luis Rio Colorado, Mexico, which is where he was living. They went with him for a week. When they returned, it seemed like they felt really sorry for their father. And I told them, "You can see your father anytime you want to, but remember, he never gave you anything, not even a little present."

That was in 1975. A year later, he called them and asked them to come see him again, and they went with a friend. Eduardo came back to California with them, but he didn't speak to me at all. He went to the restaurant with the children, and a friend picked him up there. He didn't seek out his children again until thirteen years later, in 1989. A lady called me at my business and asked for Gloria's home phone number. She said she was a friend of Gloria's, and it turns out that it was Eduardo, my daughters' father! And do you know what? Neither one wanted to see him. They were already married, and each one had three children. Gloria and Esmeralda called to ask me what to do. I said that their father wanted to see them. What else could I do? I said, "He's your father. It's up to you to see him or not."

Well, they decided to see him. He spent three days in their homes. He met his grandchildren and he has never returned. I think he's still alive. We haven't heard anything for more than five years. Now I think that if I found decent men, perhaps I wouldn't have done all these things I worked so hard at so I could give my family a better future. Maybe Gloria wouldn't have become a teacher, nor Rafael a doctor. You really have to be very willing to work hard to pay for your children's education and to think positively. Because if you ever say that you can't, well, you can't. But if you say, "I can," then you can. You can for sure! There are some negative people. As some of my friends used to say to me, "You're killing yourself working so that your kids can go to the university. Do you really think they're studying? A lot of kids just say they're going to study, and what they do is have fun and get involved with the wrong things."

If I had paid attention to those negative things, Gloria wouldn't be a teacher and Rafael wouldn't be a doctor. When I began the restaurant business, I lot of people thought I was foolish, even crazy. They thought I didn't know what I was doing. Some people came to my restaurant just to laugh at me because they didn't believe I knew how to do it. If I had paid attention to them, I'd still be at the Foster Farms plant, working with chickens. And I'd probably have rheumatism! Now a lot of people tell me that I've been very lucky. I think so, too, but I had to seek out that luck. It didn't come easily. I had to cry from exhaustion before it came, and I didn't just sit around waiting for luck.

My Recipe for Success

I want to give a message to people who aren't happy with what they are doing and who want to change and get ahead. Never pay attention to negative things. There is one extremely important point: you have to know what you want to do and how far you want to go. And if you really want something, you can achieve it. I'm nobody to be giving advice, nor do I consider myself the best example in the world. Nevertheless, I'm going to give you the recipe I used to get where I wanted to be. I've never stopped smiling. Even though I was crying inside, I was laughing on the outside. But you also have to have a lot of courage. If not, you can never get where you want to be.

We always have to see things positively and not allow ourselves to be stopped by the obstacles on the road of life. Even better, we need to keep dreaming about positive, happy things and set new goals for ourselves. If something bad has happened to us, we have to remedy it as well as we can; and if we can't, forget it because we can't change the past. But we can try to change in the present to improve our future. We don't have to carry the past around with us. No matter how much it bothers, hurts, or worries us, we have to try to leave the past in the past and enjoy our happy moments, even if they're very brief.

I want to tell people who have worked very hard and have made sacrifices in order to get ahead and become famous in what they are doing that they shouldn't allow fame and money to make them cruel and egotistic because being famous means being very careful. It's much more responsibility, and you probably have to work much harder than when you weren't famous and nobody trusted you. It's very important to keep your good reputation. If you don't, everything you earned with so much work and sacrifice can go up in smoke. Fame and responsibility always go hand in hand. Don't forget it. Both things require a lot of attention and hard work.

And if you're depressed because of one of those loved ones who can kill you, don't let yourself die. Fight to rid of that depression. Why let yourself die because of somebody who doesn't love you and probably isn't worth it? Don't humiliate yourself by begging that person to come back to you. If that person loves you, he'll look for you; and if not, let him go. It's just not worth it to fight for an impossible unrequited love! If that happened to you and you couldn't take a short vacation, do you know what you could do? Plant flowers around your house! Or talk to a friend who understands you and doesn't criticize you. Decorate your house. That also helps. Or go window-shopping in all the stores in your town. It doesn't cost anything to look.

One more effective thing—the best—is to search for God. Study the Bible wholeheartedly and with a lot of faith. Bars and discotheques won't help you if you are disillusioned, unless you have a really good friend to go with you. Otherwise, if you go to a disco alone, look for distraction because you are very sad and disillusioned. I'm sure you'll very quickly find somebody who wants to console you and will sweet talk you and later cause you more problems than you already have. That's reality! I lived through all those experiences and I always say that love is the most beautiful thing in the world. But how it hurts when it's only one-sided! You give your all and get nothing back, but that's the way life is. We're never happy with ourselves. Something always seems to be lacking.

My Future Plans

When I started writing this book, I was planning Erica's fifteenth birthday party, which took place in November 1995. Erica wants to be a performing artist, and I am going to help her study in her chosen field.

Now my future plans are, first of all, to take care of my business and keep my tax information in good shape. And every time that I can, I want to take vacations to countries I've never been to. I would also like to bring some happiness to old people who have nobody to visit them, and the same for orphan children. I am looking for things I can do for them. I'm sure that I'm going to find a way to bring them a little happiness.

Finally, I continue to ask God for strength, energy, health, knowledge, and patience to never let me be selfish and to allow me to keep smiling and to continue to love the people who surround me. May God bless all humankind and may He keep my children on the right road. I am very grateful to God for giving me the energy and the opportunity to write the story of my life. I hope that this story can help people with needs—especially for love!

Why My Story?

I always thought that one day, I would write the story of my life, but I didn't do it sooner because of so much work and responsibility. Besides, first I had to make my dreams come true. I started to write it down twenty-four years ago. I wrote forty pages and kept them with the idea of continuing someday. When I moved from Delhi to Turlock, I threw out a lot of things I no longer needed and I didn't realize that my forty pages were among those things.

Well, have you heard of Thalia, the heroine of the soap opera *Marimar*? I really don't have time to watch the soaps, but I liked that story very much. And since it was on at 9:00 p.m., I often had time to watch it. The night the last episode was on, I was watching it with my daughter Erica. It was on March 6, 1995. I said to Erica, "Oh, honey, that was great! I liked the story."

But that was just a made-up story. She didn't really go through all those things, and I really lived an incredible soap opera life. I stated telling Erica how I had come from Mexico with three small children. I don't know why but I began to laugh and cry; when Erica saw me crying, tears also began to roll down her cheeks. I said to her, "Now I'm really going to begin to write my story."

The next day, March 7, 1995, I began to write the story down. I hope that what I lived through can help people who no longer want to live because of failed loves or businesses and who think they are failures. Just think, it's never too late to start over. The only time it's too late is when you die; death is the only thing that can't be changed. And for those who are in love but aren't loved back, don't commit suicide or allow yourselves to die. There are a lot of beautiful reasons in the world to keep on living. You just have to look for them. Why should we take our own lives? Why should we get involved with anything that won't help us at all and instead only destroys us?

Finally, I want to say that after many years of hard work, I remember all the times that I felt like dropping everything and going off to the hills to be eaten by lions because I felt like I couldn't keep going. But you see, I never did it. One thing is to think about it, another is to do something that we will later regret and not be able to change.

This is the end of my story up until now. I still have a lot to do with God's help. I think everybody who has supported me with my business in the past, such as Gary Condit, whose invitation to Washington DC really benefited our business. And thanks as well to everybody who has helped me under difficult circumstances. And thanks also to those who hurt me. Why not? They taught me about bad things, but I fought hard to change those things into something better. And many, many thanks to all my clients who have enjoyed my food and have supported me for twenty-five years. And a million thanks to God for the immense strength, health, and life that He has given me. For my children, who are my life, and for the joy that I have known in this life.

La familia!

WE WOULD LIKE TO BRING the readers up to date on the lives of Lupe and her five children since the original book was published in 1999.

Erica, Lupe's youngest daughter, has founded three successful preschools, taught early childhood education, and is currently a kindergarten teacher. She works at a private Christian school where her son, Elisha, attends and is involved in a wide range of extracurricular activities. Erica's husband, Matt, is the superintendent of the school. They enjoy the opportunity of working together every day. Her relationship with her father has been reconciled.

Javier continues to work alongside his mom, Lupe, at their latest (and largest) La Morenita Restaurant. Javier has expanded into a very successful catering business. He has three wonderful children—Josiah, Noah, and Zoe—and five dogs. Javier and Deanna do a great job co-parenting. Javier enjoys life to the full and keeps up with all the kids and their sports activities. Always up for a trip or a party, Javier lives wild at heart.

Ralph was recruited back to The University of California, San Francisco (UCSF) where he has led national research and public health efforts to reduce the overuse of antibiotics. He has developed a training curriculum and certificate program in Implementation Science. In 2008, he and his family moved to Cuernavaca, Mexico, for a sabbatical year at the Instituto Nacional de Salud Pública, where he designed and implemented a careful antibiotic use program as a Fulbright scholar. He currently serves as the Chief Innovation Officer for UCSF Health. His wife, Elizabeth, works as a dietician in a cardiology practice. They have three amazing children—Michael, Maya, and Izzy—and two rescue dogs. The family resides in Kentfield, California, where they enjoy all the benefits of the beautiful outdoors.

Ralph is an avid runner and continues to participate in local races, marathons, and ultramarathons.

Esmeralda (Mary) and her husband, Jorge, went on to start their own very successful chain of Mexican food restaurants called El Jardin. They opened locations in Santa Cruz, California, Tuolumne County, and throughout the Central Valley of California. They have four children—Chasity, Nicole, Ezekiel, and Zephaniah. In their young married years, Jorge and Mary served as missionaries. Currently they are pastoring a local church and still overseeing several El Jardin outlets. They live in Twain Harte, California. They have eleven grandchildren and just celebrated their forty-year wedding anniversary.

Gloria finished her degree in English Literature. She and Mark taught in the public schools for a short time while also working in a local church as youth pastors. They went on to open their own La Morenita in 1994. Sadly, in 2009, Mark passed away unexpectedly. He will forever be missed. In honor of Mark's life, the family went on to open a new restaurant in 2011. La Mo Cafe has enjoyed much success introducing many new recipes (using locally sourced ingredients) from Spain, Cuba, and Latin America. In keeping with Mark's passion for coffee, a specialty coffee shop was added to the restaurant in 2014. Mark and Gloria have five children—Brityn, Hillary, Jordan, Robbie, and Audrey. They have four grandchildren.

Lupe will be celebrating her eightieth birthday this year. She continues to go to work every day to ensure the quality of food remains true to her recipes. Her many lifelong customers are like *familia* to Lupe. At last count, there were over thirty Mexican restaurants using Lupe's recipes. She is a constant source of inspiration to many and is frequently asked to share her story at schools and events. In spite of all the challenges she has faced, Lupe has kept her positive outlook in life and her easy laugh. She still resides in her dream house with her constant companion, her sister Albina. She is always up for an adventure (a Mexican film company just finished shooting several scenes at Lupe's beautiful home and restaurant for an upcoming big screen movie)…or a quick trip to the casino with all her *amigas*.

Left to right:
Ralph, Mary Esmeralda, Gloria, Lupe, Javier, Erica.

Back row L-R
George, Ralph, Harvey, Matt
Front row L-R
Deanna, Beth, Lupe, Gloria, Mary (Esmeralda), Érica

GUADALUPE CORDOBA

Glossary

THE FOLLOWING LIST INCLUDES WORDS that were left in Spanish in the text of the translation for the following reasons: some have no convenient direct translations; others convey the flavor of the story more completely when left in Spanish; and still others are titles of songs, names of places, and nicknames for people.

Atole. a thick, porridge-like Mexican drink made with a cornmeal base.

Cinco de Mayo. Mexican holiday commemorating the defeat of French troops in Puebla on May 5, 1862

Comal. originally a thin clay disk used for cooking corn tortillas; currently the comal may be cast iron

Coyote. basic referent to the animal; in colloquial speech, it is the person who illegally transports aliens to the United States

Curandera. local healer

Diente de oro. golden tooth; the title of a popular Mexican song

El Norte. north; colloquially, the United States

gas oil. a kind of fuel used in Diesel engines; commonly used in lamps in rural Mexico

Gema. gem, the title of a popular Mexican song

Guare. typical dress used by the indigenous people of Michoacán, Mexico

Guayabillas. tropical fruit, small sweet guavas

La Macarena. name of a dance popularized in the 1990s

La Morenita. diminutive form for *morena* or brunette; name given to Lupe Cordoba's restaurants; also Lupe Cordoba's nickname

La Pelona. bald or shaved head; nickname of one of Lupe Cordoba's employers

Las Mananitas. song typically played for the celebration of a birthday or a Saint's day

Mariachi. typical Mexican musical group featuring guitars, violins, trumpets, and other instruments

Marimar. name of a popular television soap opera shown on Spanish language television channels

Me tate. stone with a concave upper surface used for grinding grains

Molcajete. stone or pottery mortar on a tripod

Donedica. little coin, name of a popular Mexican song

Posadas. Christmas celebration in which participants emulate the story of Mary and Joseph, going from house to house seeking shelter until they are finally admitted to one of the houses

Pazole. stew of young corn, meat, and chili

Quinceanera. Typical fifteenth birthday part; somewhat similar to the "sweet sixteen" parties of the English-speaking world

Sopes. thick, cooked cornmeal, similar to tortillas, eaten separately or used to soak up other juicy foods

Sopita. a small amount of soup, a diminutive form of sope

Taquitos. small crisp tacos filled with meat and spices

Tostadas. crisp bits of tortilla; also a dish made with a crisp tortilla base and filled with meat, lettuce, beans, and spices

About the Author

GUADALUPE CORDOBA WISHES TO CONVEY the significant role that faith in God, respect and love for others, and hard work can play in helping one accomplish goals and acquire dreams, as shown in her first published book, *La Morenita: The Story of Lupe Cordoba*. In these pages, she shares her struggles and successes with the hope of encouraging and inspiring others.

Born in Michoacán, Mexico, Cordoba has made her home in Turlock, California, for more than thirty years. A self-employed restaurant owner, she is an active member of the Hispanic Chamber of Commerce, dozens of local charitable organizations, and a variety of sports clubs and teams. She also enjoys gardening and traveling. Cordoba has raised five children: Gloria, Mary, Ralph, Javier, and Erica.

CPSIA information can be obtained
at www.ICGtesting.com
Printed in the USA
FSHW011705170921
84823FS